THE MYSTERIES OF HOMER'S GREEKS

Also by I. G. EDMONDS

Allah's Oil: Mideast Petroleum
China's Red Rebel: The Story of Mao Tse-Tung
D.D. Home: The Man Who Talked with Ghosts
Ethiopia: Land of the Conquering Lion of Judah
The Khmers of Cambodia: The Story of a Mysterious People
The Magic Brothers: Carl and Alexander Herrmann
The Magic Makers: Magic and the Men Who Made It
The Magic Man: The Life of Robert-Houdin
Mao's Long March
Micronesia: Pebbles in the Sea
The Mysteries of Troy
The New Malaysia
Pakistan: Land of Mystery, Tragedy and Courage
Second Sight: People Who Read the Future
Taiwan: The Other China
Thailand, the Golden Land
The United Nations

THE MYSTERIES OF HOMER'S GREEKS

by I.G. Edmonds

Elsevier/Nelson Books
New York

To ANNETTE, beloved daughter

Map by Ellen LoGiudice

Library of Congress Cataloging in Publication Data

Edmonds, I G
  The mysteries of Homer's Greeks.

  Bibliography: p.
  Includes index.
  SUMMARY: Presents myths and facts about the
earliest Greek-speaking civilization, which came to the
Plain of Argos over 3500 years ago.
    1. Civilization, Mycenaean.   [1. Civilization,
Mycenaean.   2. Mythology, Greek]   I. Title.
DF220.E32   938'.01   80-24014
ISBN 0-525-66692-3

Published in the United States by Elsevier/Nelson
Books, a division of Elsevier-Dutton Publishing Com-
pany, Inc., New York. Published simultaneously in Don
Mills, Onrario, by Nelson/Canada.

Printed in the U.S.A.   First Edition
10   9   8   7   6   5   4   3   2   1

Contents

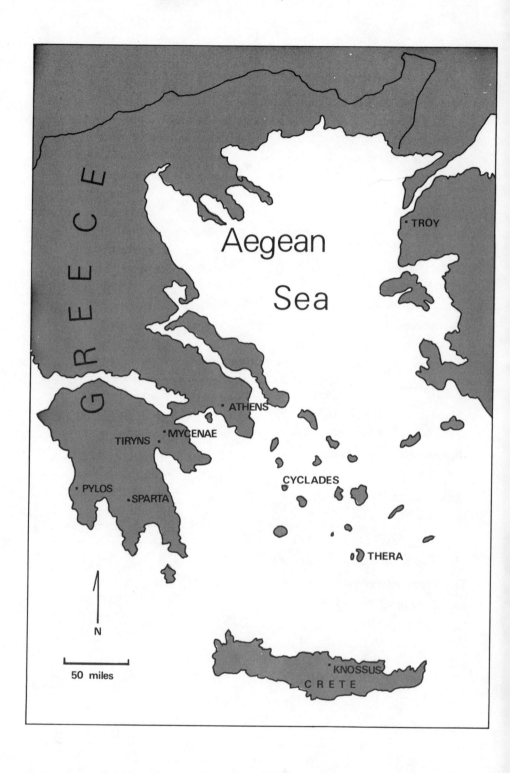

Introduction

When we think of Greece most of us picture the Parthenon, sitting in ancient splendor atop the Acropolis overlooking Athens. We think of Pericles, Alcibiades, Xenophon, and Leonidas, the great names of Classical Greece. We recall giant literary figures like Euripides, Sophocles, Thucydides, and Aeschylus. We admire the art of Phidias and the philosophy of Socrates, Plato, and Aristotle.

This was the Golden Age of Greece, and it deserves our awe and admiration. However, there is another and more ancient Greece. It is so old that the people of Classical Greece looked upon its ruins with the same awe and admiration we give today to them.

This land and its people, who were ancient to the Greeks we call ancient today, are the Mycenaeans. They lived on the Plain of Argos, which lies roughly between Corinth and Sparta in the Peloponnesus sector of Greece. The people are called Mycenaean after the great citadel of Mycenae, which tops a 900-foot hill between Mount Prophet Elias and Mount Zara in the center of the Plain of Argos.

Although prehistoric tribes lived in the Argolid as far back as 20,000 B.C., the first Greek-speaking people did not arrive until about 1700 B.C. The newcomers were a hungry, nomadic people who came from central Europe seeking food. Overnight, apparently, they changed from barbarians into a remarkably civilized people. The change came so suddenly that it seems certain that some highly civilized people taught them. But there were no such people in the Argolid at that time.

The Mycenaeans lived in the Heroic Age of Greece, producing men later worshiped as gods or demigods. They traced their ancestry back only one or two generations to the gods themselves. This may indicate that the Greek gods originated in deified heroes, men who earlier led these people in their migrations. In fact, the citadel of Mycenae was said to have been founded by Perseus, son of Zeus and Danaë, who is famed in mythology for slaying the snake-haired Medusa whose glance turned men to stone.

Mycenae is also the land of Heracles (Hercules), the muscular demi-god, and of the Greeks who destroyed Troy. This is the reason we call these people Homer's Greeks. Actually Homer lived five hundred years after the fall of Mycenae, but, his epic poem, the *Iliad*, depicts the Mycenaeans so graphically that for nearly three thousand years entranced readers have seen these people as Homer described them. Although he never knew them personally, Agamemnon of Mycenae, Menelaus of Sparta, and the other heroes are truly Homer's Greeks, for his genius made them so.

There is no lack of stories about Mycenae and the mighty people who lived there, but the truth has become interwoven with legend and mythology. Then the great playwrights of Classical Greece further distorted the legends in their plays. It is not proper, however, to dismiss the latter-day legends, plays, stories, and epic poetry as complete fiction. Over the years archaeological discoveries have proved a fact here and there. For example, Homer in the *Iliad* tells of Nestor, king of Pylos, drinking from a golden cup. The cup was described as two-handled, with tiny golden doves fashioned on top of the handles. Heinrich Schliemann, digging in the ruins of Mycenae, found a golden cup exactly fitting this description. It can now be seen in the Mycenaean Hall of the National Archaeological Museum in Athens. This and other discoveries caused one writer to remark, "Homer knew whereof he spoke."

Mycenae was a mystery to the Greeks of the Classical Age, and it is still a mystery to us today. No one knows where the Mycenaean invaders of Peloponnesus came from. How they became civilized so suddenly is another mystery. How they were able to build fortifications so tremendous that latter-day Greeks said that mere men could not have done it, they had to have been built by the Cyclopes—giants sent by Zeus. What the Mycenaeans really did in the famous Trojan War is another mystery. The final fall of Mycenae and what happened to its people has never been explained either.

However, over a hundred years of patient digging in the ruins of the Mycenaean cities has produced some pieces of the historical jigsaw, solving some of the mysteries of Homer's Greeks but revealing still more mysteries at the same time. This century has also packed the Mycenaean Hall in the National Archaeological museum in Athens with awesome treasure from this long-ago people.

The people of Mycenae were brilliant architects, as their beehive tombs and mighty walls show. They were brave and powerful warriors, as we learn from the legends. They were vicious and extraordinarily cruel in their revenge, as the playwrights reveal to us. But they were also very human, as Homer records in the *Iliad*.

A more fascinating people never lived in any age than these heroes we call Homer's Greeks. And equally fascinating are the brilliant, bull-headed, and often quarrelsome people of the nineteenth and twentieth centuries who pushed back the shadows of the years to throw so much light on these wonderful people who came to the Plain of Argos over 3,500 years ago.

This is the story of both.

1

THE THIEF FROM TROY

Heinrich Schliemann might have been mistaken for a timid clerk by people seeing him at a distance. He was a small man with receding hair. Large round glasses gave him a goggle-eyed appearance. His voice was high-pitched. But underneath this misleading exterior was the soul of a lion and the temper of a tyrant. Anything and anybody who stood in the way of Schliemann's ambitions were obstacles to be destroyed.

One of the roadblocks to his ambitions was a slender, excitable Greek named Panagiotis Stamatakis. Schliemann thought Stamatakis a quarrelsome idiot, and the Greek thought Schliemann a vicious viper and a colossal thief.

As for the accusation of thief, Stamatakis was right. Schliemann stole the gold of Troy, a treasure trove so fabulous that it is impossible to put a price upon it.

Now Schliemann was digging into the ruins of Mycenae. The Greek government feared that the crafty little man intended to steal whatever of value he found in the Mycenaean ruins. Stamatakis had been detailed to watch over the German archaeologist and see that all treasure trove went to the Greek museums.

A marble bust of Heinrich Schliemann sits at the door of the Mycenaean Hall in Athens' National Archaeological Museum, where the treasures he found are on display.

Stamatakis was also instructed to see that Schliemann, in his zeal to find treasure, did not destroy any of the existing walls of the ancient citadel. Schliemann was not a trained archaeologist. He worked largely by intuition. If he decided to dig in a certain spot, he did so. He did not care what was in the way. So, his orders to the foreman of his diggers would often bring Stamatakis running up to cry, "Stop!"

Then Schliemann would fly into a rage. He would scream at the unfortunate Greek and shake his fist in the man's face. Stamatakis' mustache would bristle, and he would shout back angrily at the furious German. After the two men had exhausted themselves with words, they would rush to their respective offices and dash off furious letters to the government in Athens.

Schliemann complained that Stamatakis was interfering with his work. He insisted that he loved Greece and was only working to uncover the glory of this great country's past; but much as he loved Greece, he could not continue working if stupid officials kept hounding him every time his workmen put a pick in the ground.

Stamatakis wrote the head the Greek Archaeological Society, a government organization that had sent him to Mycenae to watch over Schliemann, that he could no longer put up with the insults of this terrible-tempered foreigner. He begged to be relieved of his arduous duties before his health was ruined. Schleimann, he insisted, was a mad tyrant.

Neither man received sympathy or aid from Athens. The Greek government distrusted Schliemann; somebody had to watch him. Unfortunately, Stamatakis, with his archaeological background, was the best man to do so. "You will stay," he was told. "If this foreigner makes off with any treasure from Mycenae as he did at Troy, you will be held strictly responsible."

Stamatakis groaned in agony when he received this reply. Schliemann wasn't happy with the letter he received either. It said only that the govornment appreciated fully the great sacrifices that the famous archaeologist was making to carry on his work at Mycenae. History would surely recognize Herr Schliemann for the great man that he was. His complaints against Stamatakis were ignored.

Government officials, thoroughly sick of the little German's constant complaints and rages, would have been happy to expel Schliemann from the country, except for two things: (1), he was a German citizen, and the German government became most unhappy when one of its citizens was mistreated. And (2), an archaeological dig is an expensive program to keep going; the government badly wanted the digging at Mycenae to continue, but it did not have the money to support it. The country was bankrupt; and Schliemann, a millionaire, was paying for all the work himself. So, the official position was this: Let the rascal continue, but watch every move he makes.

Despite his threats to leave, Schliemann had no intention of doing so. He and Stamatakis would then get together, shake hands, assure each other of their mutual respect, and pledge to work harmoniously for the good of the project. Such truces rarely lasted longer than two days, and then the two men would be screaming at each other again and writing more furious complaints to Athens.

At times Schliemann got discouraged and considered abandoning the dig. But he was a stubborn man, and shortly his stubbornness would be rewarded with a stunning discovery that would shed new light on the mysterious men of Mycenae.

The long road that finally led Heinrich Schliemann to Greece began in Mecklenburg, Germany, where he was born in 1822. When he was seven, his father, pastor of a small church, gave him a copy of Ludwig Jerrer's *Illustrated History of the World*. In it was a picture of the fall of Troy. Young Heinrich was enthralled.

He begged his father to tell him about it. In the days that followed, Pastor Schliemann told his son the entire history of Troy and the Trojan War: Paris, prince of Troy, stole Helen, wife of Menelaus, king of Sparta. Then the vengeful Greeks under Agamemnon, king of Mycenae, besieged Troy. The war went on for ten years. Then Odysseus, later hero of the *Odyssey*, suggested a trick. The Greeks appeared to give up and leave, abandoning a giant wooden horse, supposedly an offering to the goddess Athena. The Trojans pulled the horse into the city, not knowing that Odysseus and some Greek soldiers were hidden inside. These men slipped out in the night, and the Greeks, who had only pretended to sail away, returned. Caught with the enemy inside and out, the Trojans were destroyed in the fighting.

Pastor Schliemann based his account of Troy's fall upon Homer's epic poem, the *Iliad*. This is an account of the last few days of the war. It tells how Agamemnon, the king of Mycenae and leader of the Greeks fighting Troy, insulted Achilles, the greatest of the Greek heroes. Sulking, Achilles withdrew himself and his men from the battle. This almost caused the Greeks to lose the war. Then, when Achilles' great friend, Patroclus, is killed by Hector, champion of the Trojans, Achilles rejoins the fighting. He kills Hector in a stirring personal duel. A twelve-day truce is declared so that both sides can bury their hero dead.

The *Iliad* ends here, before the acutal fall of Troy. Pastor Schliemann told the story so well that his son fell in love with the Trojans. The boy was crushed to learn that the site of Troy had been forgotten. Some even claimed that there never had been such a place. It was all a great poet's invention.

Young Schliemann refused to believe this. He told his father that, when he became a man, he would search for and find Troy.

The family fell on hard times when Heinrich was a teenager. Pastor Schliemann was dismissed from his church for marrying a servant girl after his wife died. The boy went to work in a store, but had to quit when he hurt himself lifting huge barrels. For the next several years he drifted from one low-paying job to another. He barely made enough to survive.

He taught himself to write and speak several foreign languages. This gave him an opportunity to go to Russia as agent for a large firm. He began branching out for himself and made a fortune. Then the California gold rush of 1849 took him to San Francisco, where he made another $600,000 banking raw gold. Finally, in 1863, he retired, a multimillionaire. He devoted the rest of his life to his dream of finding Troy.

In the meantime, he had grown to love all things Grecian. He read his copy of the *Iliad* every day. It was not an epic poem to him. He looked upon every word that Homer wrote as exact history.

He went to Turkey, where Troy was supposed to have been, surveying the area with a copy of Homer's poem in his hand. Homer said that Mount Ida was visible from Troy. He sought places where he could see the mountain. Homer said there was a river nearby and that it was close to the seashore. Schliemann searched out every geographical reference in the *Iliad* and kept searching until he found a place that fitted them all.

This turned out to be Hissarlik, a mound four miles from the shore of the Aegean Sea near the mouth of the Hellespont (the present Dardanelles, the narrow strait leading from the Aegean Sea into the Sea of Marmara).

Schliemann's faith in Homer was so great that he got permission from the Turkish government to dig in the Hissarlik mound. To everyone's astonishment except his own, he discovered that the mound hid the ruins of nine cities. Each had been destroyed at some point and another built atop the ruins.

Since the ruins in Layer Two showed signs of having been burned, Schliemann decided that this was the city of the Trojan War. It was not until 1935 that the city of the *Iliad* was proved to be Layer Seven.

Schliemann was watching his diggers one day in the early summer of 1873. As they uncovered dirt in a hole near Troy II's walls, his sharp eye caught the yellow glint of gold. He hastily dismissed the workers, telling them he had decided to give them a holiday because of their hard work.

Then, at great risk to himself, he and the Greek girl he had recently married climbed down into the hole and dug out the gold with a knife. It proved to be a fabulous treasure, including a diadem, necklace, and earrings that could only have been worn by a queen of Troy.

They wrapped the treasure in Sophia Schliemann's shawl and smuggled it back to their cottage. Later Schliemann smuggled it out to Greece. Under his agreement with the Turkish government, all finds were to have been shared between Schliemann and the National Museum in Istanbul. But Schliemann did not intend to part with any piece of this treasure. This was the gold of Troy—the city of his dreams, he thought. That necklace may once have graced the neck of Helen herself or perhaps Andromache, the beloved wife of the hero Hector. Share it with the Turks? Never! He was not concerned with the value of the treasure. He already had more money than he could ever spend. He wanted it because it came from Troy.

Unfortunately for him, in his haste he overlooked two gold pieces.

Some of the workmen found them after Schliemann returned to Greece. One gave an earring to his wife. She wore it in public, and the government found out about it. They knew then that Schliemann had stolen some Trojan treasure, although they did not know how fabulous his find was.

They demanded the Trojan gold be returned. Schliemann angrily refused. The Turks sued him in the Greek courts. To hedge against losing, Schliemann split the treasure into five parts and hid them in different sections of Greece; thus he hoped to keep the authorities from finding all of it.

As the case dragged on, Schliemann became restless. He wanted desperately to get back to his dig at Troy, but the Turks naturally would not let him resume digging until he returned the stolen relics. This he did not intend to do.

One day Schliemann was reading Pausanias, the second-century A.D. Greek who wrote *Descriptions of Greece*, an account of his visit to the ruins of his time. He was suddenly struck by something Pausanias said about Mycenae:

> Some remains of the circuit wall are still to be seen, and the gate which has the lions over it. These were built, they say, by the Cyclopes, who made the walls of Tiryns.
> There is a tomb of Atreus [father of Agamemnon] and his children where their treasures are kept. There is the tomb of those whom Aegisthus slew at the banquet, on their return from Troy with Agamemnon. . . . There is also the tomb of Agamemnon. . . . Clytemnestra and Aegisthus were buried a little way outside the wall, for they were thought not worthy to be within, where Agamemnon lay and those who fell with him.

Schliemann read this with growing excitement. Pausanias was referring to the tragedy that followed Agamemnon's return from the Trojan War. He and his close followers were killed by his enemy Aegisthus, with the cooperation of Agamemnon's faithless wife, Clytemnestra. Aegisthus then took the throne of Mycenae.

What excited Schliemann was the possibility of finding another treasure from ancient times, as he had done at Troy. He knew that it was the custom to bury a king's treasures in the grave with him. Pausanias placed Agamemnon's grave inside the city walls and those of Queen Clytemnestra and King Aegisthus just outside the walls.

Schliemann had great faith in the old Greek writers. He accepted Pausanias' statements as truth, just as he had earlier sworn by every line of Homer.

A few years before, he had visited Mycenae but had not been overly impressed. But now he was inspired by the hope of finding the tomb of the men who had led the Greeks against Troy. During a break in the trial with the Turks, he and Sophia made a trip to Mycenae. They went first to Nauplia, a city on the Gulf of Argos, and took horses from there for the fifteen-mile ride to Mycenae.

The plain of Argos as it appears from inside the Mycenae Citadel walls. The Lion Gate is below the wall of stones at the right.

Mycenae is situated on a hill that rises about 160 feet above the plain, guarding the pass between Mount Prophet Elias and Mount Zara. A stone wall circles the top of the hill, where the rich king's palace and government buildings were located. About halfway down the hill, another wall encircles the inner city, where the people and the nobility lived. Below this, the ordinary city stretched down the hill and into the plain.

The ruins were little changed from the days of Pausanias. Since Pausanias made a point of mentioning "the gate which has the lions over it," Schliemann went directly to this location. This is the famous Lion Gate.

The gate is a break in the walls of the inner city. Here there is an outcropping of jutting rock. The builders of the wall rolled huge boulders into place atop this rock. No attempt was made to dress the stones and fit them together. They were put in place and the spaces between them stuffed with smaller rocks and clay to make a tremendous wall. A second wall was built parallel to this and the spaces between the stones stuffed with rocks and rubble to make a solid wall that averages from 15 to 18 feet thick. This wall was so strongly constructed that almost all of it remains to this day.

The size of the stones convinced later Greeks that the walls could only have been built by giants. They attributed the work to the Cyclopes, a mythological race of one-eyed giants living in Sicily. (This belief has given the term "cyclopean" to this type of construction.) The placement of the huge stone atop the naked living rock, jutting from the hill, makes it appear as if the wall itself were growing from the earth.

At the northwest corner of the inner city walls, the fortifications cut inward to create a narrow bastion that guards the main entrance, the Lion Gate. It was constructed in this way so that warriors on the walls could hurl rocks and spears down upon any invader who pierced the main city walls and reached the inner city.

The Lion Gate itself is about ten feet high and six feet wide at the bottom, narrowing slightly at the top. A huge shaped stone has been placed across the top to make a lintel. Then, to keep the massive weight of the wall above from pressing too hard upon the lintel, a large

The Lion gate is at the right. The famous carving is on the opposite side of the triangular stone above the lintel. The Granary is the wall of stone behind the visitors in the lower center of the picture. The slabs of the grave circle appear in the lower left corner.

triangular stone was placed on top of the lintel to relieve the pressure. It is carved with the figures of two lions in relief. Their front feet are raised on a pedestal, and they face each other. The heads have been missing since before Pausanias' day. The gate owes its fame not only to the rough beauty of the relief, but also to the fact that it is the earliest known example of ancient Greek monumental sculpture.

Holes in the lintel and in the base show that huge posts were used to open and close the massive doors.

Inside the gate, the walls opened into a half circle. A straight road led directly to a ramp that curved to become a road leading to the acropolis on top of the hill. Inside the half circle, where the wall bulged out, there was a ring of stone slabs, many broken. Between this ring and the wall by the gate were ruins of a building now called the Granary, because some bottles containing carbonized grain were found in it. It was probably a house for the gate guards. Beyond the slab ring, Schliemann found debris that seemed to hide house walls.

Schliemann and Sophia climbed to the top of the acropolis. Much of the wall was still in place, but only rubble indicated where the castle had been. While his young wife rested from the climb, Schliemann scrambled up on the acropolis wall. For a long time he stared down at the Lion Gate and the terrace just inside the gate.

Beyond the lower walls he could pick out evidence of the lower city where the commoners had lived. When Sophia joined him, Schliemann waved his hand in a gesture to include the area below the gate.

"Somewhere in there Clytemnestra is buried," he said. "And Aegisthus' tomb is nearby. Perhaps they are side by side."

Then he pointed to the stone circle inside the Lion Gate. "And somewhere in there is the tomb of Agamemnon."

He did not say that the tomb *might* be there. Pausanias had written that the great king's tomb was inside the walls. That was enough for Schliemann. There were only two questions in his mind: Exactly where was the king buried? And had the tomb been robbed since Pausanias saw it 1,700 years earlier?

Schliemann was careful in his business dealings but impulsive in his archaeological work. He decided to dig in Mycenae. He asked no permission, just hired some diggers and set them to cutting a ditch across the terrace inside the Lion Gate. This was the same technique he had used at Troy. A deep ditch straight across would permit him to sample the entire area. Then, if something interesting was revealed, he would come back to this portion for expanded work.

Word reached Athens of his high-handed takeover. Officials were rushed out from Nauplia to stop him. Schliemann fumed and raged. He pointed out, with some justification, that no one else had thought enough of Mycenae to dig there. He saw no reason why he should be disturbed by meddlesome officials.

The Nauplia people had orders to be as polite as possible, for, after all, Schliemann was a very rich and very famous man. But he was not to dig anymore until he had received permission from Athens.

Taking Sophia with him, Schliemann stalked off in a rage. He declared that he was leaving Greece forever. He was only trying to uncover the heritage of the country, and all the thanks he got for it was to be treated as a thief and a knave.

However, he had no intention of abandoning Mycenae or Greece. The interference only whetted his desire to investigate the ruins. He set out for Athens to get official permission—and what came out of it was a truly astonishing discovery, startling everyone.

2

THE MASKS OF MYCENAE

In Athens Heinrich Schliemann received his *firman*, or official permission, to excavate in Mycenae. In order to get it, he had to agree to humiliating terms—at least he considered them humiliating. A dozen times during the negotiation he stormed out, crying he would never spend another cent to help the Greeks uncover their history. But in the end he always came back. Although Troy, now closed to him by the angry Turks, was his first love, Schliemann had become obsessed with the idea that he could find ancient treasure in Mycenae.

At Troy he had destroyed much of the later material in his eagerness to get down to the layers he thought contained the Troy of Homer. The Greek government laid down an ironclad stipulation that he could pull down no walls at Mycenae. A government inspector from the Archaeological Society would be put in as overseer to inspect all finds. All objects of archaeological value had to be turned over to the National Museum. Schliemann could keep nothing. He would be permitted to publish his finds and could take full scientific credit for the work. He would pay all expenses.

The work began in August 1874. Schliemann had no intention of abiding by any of the rules if he could help it. Instead of digging in one place, he divided his sixty-three workmen and put them to digging in so many areas that Stamatakis and his two assistants could not watch them all. The Greek archaeologist objected. Schliemann replied with screams and curses. Stamatakis complained to Athens. An order came back for Schliemann to dig in only one place at a time.

The impatient little German flew into another rage, threatening to stop all work and leave. But the Greeks had heard all that many times before, and Stamatakis told Schliemann that he would be delighted if the German left. Schliemann dashed off to write another letter to Athens, demanding that the Greek inspector be removed and a sensible replacement sent to Mycenae.

Stamatakis wrote another letter of his own. He complained bitterly this time that Schliemann insisted on sorting the day's finds each night, working until two or three o'clock in the morning. The Greek had to stay with him or risk being cheated. This meant as much as eighteen to twenty hours a day on the job. Schliemann, a much older man, thrived on the long hours, but Stamatakis claimed his health was being undermined. He begged to be replaced.

Athens had received so many letters from both men that they were all treated as jokes now.

Schliemann, after considering all possible places to dig seriously, decided on the rubble-covered house foundations near the stone circle. He mistakenly thought this was a royal palace. Many objects were found—stone axes, household implements, and other interesting but not particularly valuable objects. Then, in the first house from the circle, he uncovered the first really important object.

This was a broken *krater* (vase), all parts of which have never been found—the celebrated Warrior Vase. The pieces have been cemented together and plain clay used to fill in the missing pieces. Today it is one of the most interesting of the exhibits in the Mycenaean Hall at the museum in Athens.

It was an excellent example of the pottery classified as Late Hellenic III-C, made from about 1200 to 1100 B.C. This pottery was made by washing foreign matter out of yellow clay. The cleaned clay was then dried, rewetted, and shaped on a potter's wheel. Before it dried completely, it was covered with a wet wash of clay, and designs were painted on with red earth colors.

It was a valuable find under any condition, but what made Schliemann so excited was the design on the vase. It showed a woman at one side waving good-bye to a line of marching soldiers. Since the style of the

A detail from the famous Warrior Vase shows a woman bidding farewell to a line of warriors marching off to battle. The costumes of the soldiers fit Homer's description of the Achaeans who attacked Troy.

pottery dated it at about the time of the Trojan War, all authorities have agreed that the pictures show how the Greeks must have dressed and armed themselves at that time.

We can pretty well consider this krater painting as almost a scene from the *Iliad* done by a contemporary artist. It is little wonder that it created a sensation when exhibited in Athens. The soldiers are dressed in short tunics, fringed at the bottom, and they carry rounded shields. They have some kind of laced foot covering, and their legs are covered to the knees. These are probably protective shielding rather than stockings, for Homer refers to "the well-greaved Achaeans." (The word "Greek" had not been coined at this time, and they called themselves Achaeans, the reason is not clear, for Achaea was only one province of Greece.) Their heads were covered by a studded helmet with a plume hanging down the back and a horn in front to catch sword blows. The protective shield was carried in the left hand, and the right carried a long spear. A wine bottle is attached to the spear.

The woman bidding them good-bye is dressed in a flowing robe with long sleeves. All the figures are painted in red against the natural yellow background of the clay. The two handles are fashioned in the form of animals' heads. A painted decorative border circles the vase above and below the warriors.

Schliemann was sure the woman was Clytemnestra bidding farewell to the soldiers marching off to fight in Troy. But, although their armor corresponds to some of Homer's descriptions of the Greeks at Troy, there is no proof that these men were going to war. They might have been setting off on a hunting trip. Nevertheless, we can safely say that this is how Agamemnon's soldiers must have looked. More beautiful and valuable treasures were yet to come from the rubble of Mycenae, but none more interesting than the Warrior Vase. To this day the place where it was found is marked on maps of Mycenae as "The House of the Warrior Vase."

This great discovery increased Schliemann's enthusiasm. He doubled the number of diggers. He drove them with the fury of an ancient king building a tomb. Schliemann's temper got worse. His fights with Stamatakis increased. There was one brief recess in their battles when both put on their best behavior. This was a visit to the dig by Dom Pedro II, emperor of Brazil. Schliemann went out of his way to impress the emperor.

A few miles from the Mycenaean citadel there is an enormous "beehive" tomb set in a hill. It is lined with rock that toes in to create a curious dome like a beehive, from which it takes its name. It is approached by a rock-lined passageway. The entrance is through a door that has a relieving triangle above it in the style of the Lion Gate. It is not carved, however.

Here in this three-thousand-year-old setting Schliemann served the visitor a luncheon. Then, before the royal party left, Schliemann gave the emperor a piece of Mycenaean pottery from the citadel dig. Stamatakis was disturbed, for he had orders that nothing should be taken from the site, but he could not get up enough courage to demand that the emperor return it, and Dom Pedro kept his souvenir.

The giant tomb where the luncheon was served is known locally as the Treasury of Atreus, from the local tradition that it is the tomb of Agamemnon's father. It is but one of several found in the area surrounding the Mycenaean citadel. Exactly as Pausanias had stated, the diggers uncovered two other beehive tombs just outside the Lion Gate wall. Schliemann was sure that these were the tombs of Clytemnestra and Aegisthus. However, later study showed that the construction of the so-called tomb of Aegisthus was more primitive. It is estimated to be at least 250 years older than the adjoining tomb.

The other tomb seems to have been that of a queen. Its treasures had long since been stolen, but Mrs. Schliemann—who directed the excavations here—found a gold comb and a few beauty aids in the rubble, which suggest that it was a woman's tomb.

Schliemann excavated to the foundations of the House of the Warrior Vase without finding anything else of great value. He now paused to consider where to dig next. It was getting late in the season, and work would have to stop during the cold and rain of winter.

Also Schliemann was about to come to terms with the Turks. He had been fined $5,000 for stealing the Trojan treasure. The fine was based upon his claim in court that the treasure was not worth $5,000. As it was still hidden, the Turks were not aware of its priceless value and thought the fine fair. Then Schliemann surprised them. He offered the Turks $25,000 instead of the $5,000 fine, provided the money was used for the benefit of the national museum in Istanbul. What he was trying to do was appease the angry officials, for he wanted to return to Troy and continue digging.

A return to Troy would prevent him from digging further in Mycenae. So he wanted to get as much done as possible before the 1876 digging season ended. After considering several sites, he chose to dig inside the circle of broken stones between the House of the Warrior Vase and the Lion Gate.

He had at first dismissed this as an *agora*, a meeting place. The stones were part of seats built for the elders to sit on during their discussions. However, he wanted to make at least one exploratory shaft into the ground before giving up for the winter. It was then mid-October, and the rains were starting. The first shaft opened up a grave containing the bones of three women and some diadems and crosses of gold.

Schliemann moved over and started another shaft. The second grave uncovered contained the body of one man and no objects of any worth. The two graves found indicated that the circle was not an agora, as Schliemann had first thought, but a royal burial ground. Another shaft was sunk and a third grave found. Like the others, it had been cut into the bedrock, and it contained the bones of three women and two men. There were a number of objects buried with them, but nothing overly exciting.

Broken stone slabs mark the boundary of Grave Circle A, where Schliemann uncovered five ancient graves within the citadel of Mycenae.

Then Grave IV was opened. It contained the bodies of three women and two men. As soon as the workmen's picks penetrated into the grave, it was clear that this was an enormously important find. One of the picks struck gold. Schliemann had turned away to talk to Sophia, but came running back when he heard Stamatakis yell excitedly for the men to stop digging.

He got down on his hands and knees at the edge of the shaft to peer down into the hole. As soon as he saw the glitter of the uncovered gold, he began to tremble. For a moment he couldn't speak, for he could see that this was no ordinary gold object. It was large and he thought he could see what looked like a nose sticking out of the dirt.

It's a mask! he thought. A life-size mask!

When he finally could control his excitement enough to talk, he sent the workmen away. Stamatakis shouted for the officer of the guard to station soldiers around the shaft.

"What are you going to do?" he asked Schliemann.

"It's a face mask," Schliemann said. "And it appears to be very thin gold. It must be removed most carefully. I can't do it myself, and neither can you. I'll get Mrs. Schliemann to do it, as she did the delicate removal at Troy."

Stamatakis' head jerked up from observing the hole. He looked sharply at Schliemann. He recalled that it had been Sophia who had smuggled the Trojan treasure back to their home while her husband diverted the attention of the Turks. He started to object, but changed his mind. He realized that a woman's delicate touch was needed to protect the precious object.

Schliemann sent one of the men to bring Sophia. He and Stamatakis, each grasping an arm, lowered her carefully into the grave. Then the two men crouched on the edge of the pit and watched anxiously as Sophia Schliemann gingerly used a small knife to remove the packed soil from around the golden object.

The young woman worked swiftly but delicately and soon had uncovered the object. It was, as Schliemann guessed, a facial mask that had been placed over the head of a man when he was buried. The heavy dirt had partially crushed it out of shape, but when she passed it up to her husband, the two men could easily make out the features. The gold of the mask had been beaten thin and was now badly crumpled. The heavy eyebrows, closed eyes, straight nose, and small grim mouth were still discernible, however.

The two men were drawn from their awed inspection of the mask by a cry from Sophia in the pit. She had discovered still another mask. When it was uncovered, it was like the other in form but different in features. The eyebrows were different, not being as bushy. The eyes, although closed, were bulging, and the V-shaped mouth was larger and less grim. Both faces showed no sign of a beard.

"This is not just a stylized representation," Schliemann told Stamatakis. "The features are different. That probably means that these are genuine portraits of real men. We are seeing here what the real men who fought against Troy looked like!"

There were three women buried with the two men, but they did not wear golden masks. Sophia was lifted out of the pit and the workmen brought back. They continued to dig, uncovering a crushed lion's mask, a *rhyton* (drinking vase) shaped like a bull's head, a gold seal ring carved with figures of four warriors, a gold arm band, and a slightly crushed gold cup.

Stamatakis took the objects as they were passed up. He passed them to Schliemann for inspection, and then they were placed on a table set up for that purpose. Soldiers stood guard around the table.

Stamatakis paid little attention to the gold cup. He handed it to Schliemann and turned back to the pit. He turned back quickly when he heard a choked cry from the little German. Schliemann was turning the cup slowly in his hand. He turned and called to Sophia, who was at the table inspecting the masks. She hurried over to her husband. Stamatakis, wondering what had caused the German's excitement, came over to join them.

"It's Nestor's cup!" Schliemann cried, turning the cup over in his hand. "See, here are the handles, and on top of the handles the two golden doves, just as Homer described it in the *Iliad*!"

Schliemann knew the *Iliad* by heart, and he began to quote from Book XI, the portion where Nestor is saved from death in battle and brought back to his quarters. Nestor was the oldest of the Greek leaders at Troy and the king of Pylos. The slave girl, fair-tressed Hecamede, whom he had captured in an earlier battle, prepared him a meal.

"She drew before them a fair table, polished well, with feet of cyanus, and thereon a vessel of bronze, with onion, for relish to the drink, and pale honey, and the grain of sacred barley, and—"

Here Schliemann paused before going on. Then he added: "—and beside it a right goodly cup, that the old man brought from home, embossed with studs of gold, and four handles there were to it, and around each two golden doves were feeding, and to the cup were two feet below."

Schliemann got carried away, as he usually did when he found something that proved the truth of Homer. Actually the wine cup did resemble Homer's description, but it was not exactly like it. The Mycenaean cup had two handles, whereas Homer's description said four. However, it was sufficiently close for the cup to be called Nestor's Cup ever since. It, and the golden masks, are in the Mycenaean Hall of the Athens museum.

One more great discovery remained to be made. This was in Shaft Grave V. Here they found the bodies of three men. One of these also wore a golden mask. This mask was the most remarkable of the three found. It was a majestic face. The eyes were closer together, the nose longer, and the mouth straighter than on the other masks. A mustache with upturned ends and a beard partially covered the face.

When Schliemann looked at the magnificent mask, he cried: "It is Agamemnon!"

There was considerable treasure buried with the king, although it could not compare with the number of golden objects found in Grave IV, where the first masks were uncovered. There were swords, vases, a cup, breastplates, a battle ax, and ribbons of gold, which had been wound around one of the corpses.

Schliemann was almost beside himself with joy. He kept telling Sophia over and over, "I have looked upon the face of Agamemnon!"

Then he sent her into Nauplia with a telegram for the Greek king. In it he said, "I announce to Your Majesty with extreme joy that I have

The golden mask that Schliemann thought was that of Agamemnon is today in the National Museum in Athens, Greece. It is life size and hammered from pure gold.

discovered tombs which tradition, echoed by Pausanias, has designated as the sepulchers of Agamemnon and his companions who were killed while at a meal. The graves were surrounded by a double circle of stone slabs. These would not have been erected unless great personages were buried here. In the tombs I found an immense treasure of the most ancient golden objects.

"These treasures alone will fill a great museum, the most wonderful in the world. For centuries to come thousands will flock to Greece to see them.

"I work only for the pure love of science. Accordingly, I have no claim on these treasures. I give them intact to Greece. God grant that these treasures may become the cornerstone of an immense national wealth.''

The telegram was somewhat exaggerated. He had found an immense treasure. It was far richer and more varied than the treasure he had found at Troy. It was one of the great discoveries of archaeology. It may well be the greatest discovery ever made in Europe, although it cannot compare with the great treasure trove found in King Tutankhamen's tomb in Egypt.

However, a great archaeological discovery depends not so much upon the monetary value of the find as upon what it reveals about history and the people of the time. Schliemann's threw considerable light upon the ancient Mycenaeans. It did not solve many of the mysteries of Homer's Greeks, but it did prove that there was some truth in the old myths and traditions.

Schliemann was wrong about the identity of the body he thought was Agamemnon. Through various dating methods, later archaeologists date the kings of the shaft graves at around 1600–1650 B.C., a good 350 years before the Greeks attacked Troy. The date of the Trojan War is controversial, but it is considered to be around 1200 B.C.

The graves revealed how Homer's Greeks buried their dead. They revealed how the soldiers dressed. The Warrior Vase is dated at 1300 B.C., closer to the time of the *Iliad*. The extent of Mycenaean art was also shown.

But at the same time, the excavations revealed new mysteries. Who were the gold-masked kings? The art revealed that Mycenae reached a high state of culture earlier than previously thought. Nestor's cup showed that Homer was correct in details of Greek life. So how much more truth is buried in the lines of the *Iliad* and the writings of the great playwrights of the Classical Age? Hundreds of questions were raised by the discovery—far more than were answered by it.

Schliemann was also indulging in grand rhetoric when he told the king that he was giving the treasure to Greece. Greece got the Mycenaean treasure solely becasue Stamatakis and fifteen Greek soldiers were there to see that Schliemann did not spirit it away. But although he was not always an admirable man in his personal dealings, Schliemann was one of the founding fathers of archaeology and all credit is due him for his great discoveries.

It was now early November, and Schliemann abandoned the dig. He was convinced that all the graves had been inside the stone circle and that no more would be found. He and Sophia returned to Athens, where he began sorting hundreds of photographs and piles of notes he had made. He also began writing his book, *Mycenae*. He did not intend to return to Mycenae, for his request to return to Troy was being favorably considered by the Turks.

However, he was badly mistaken in writing off Mycenae as a worked-out dig. Although there were to be no other great dramatic treasure finds, Mycenae had many more secrets to reveal. Schliemann was indirectly responsible for one of them.

While working on his notes, he decided that he did not have enough information to make a map of the site. He sent Vasilios Drosinos, a young engineer who had worked with him before, back to Mycenae to survey the area for the map.

Stamatakis, who trusted no one connected with Schliemann, went along. They had earlier discovered some carved tombstones in the grave circle. Now Drosinos found a stone as he was surveying in the vicinity of the House of the Warrior Vase. He thought that it resembled the grave-circle headstones and mentioned it to Stamatakis.

The Greek inspector was far from being the idiot that Schliemann called him. He recognized the importance of the stone and called a guard to bring a pick. The three men dug around the stone and soon uncovered a gold cup. Other cups, rings, and a sword handle came to light. Two of the rings were signets. One in particular was extraordinary.

This signet ring, although only one inch across, was carved to represent some women giving an offering to a goddess. Behind the goddess was a tree—probably an olive—and a woman was picking fruit from it. Above the women's head were two double-bladed axes. At the very top were carvings of the sun and moon side by side. Below them were some wavy lines.

Schliemann, when he saw the signet, thought the sun, moon, and lines resembled the design that Homer said Hephaestus (Vulcan), the armorer of the gods, hammered into the shield he made for Achilles. He quoted the lines to Sophia:

"Therein the shield he fashioned much cunning work. He wrought the earth, and the heavens, and the sea, and the unwearying sun, and the moon waxing to the full. . . ."

The women were bare-breasted and were dressed from the waist down in long flounced skirts that ended at the ankles.

The whole design was an extraordinary job of miniature craftsmanship. The delicacy of execution and composition made it a genuine artistic masterpiece.

The action and objects were clear enough, except for six curious designs along the left border, irregular shapes that have defied nearly a hundred years of analysis. No one has ever advanced even a tenable theory as to what they are. Schliemann said they looked like breadfruit he had seen in South America. But before we can accept this explanation, it would have to be explained how breadfruit, a tropical tree, got to Greece, and why there is no other record of it.

In addition to being a gem of art, the curious signet was the first clue as to who the people were who taught civilization to the barbaric Greek-speaking nomads who migrated to the Plain of Argos sometime between 2000 and 1600 B.C.

However, no one recognized this clue at the time. It lay in the double axes, the bare breasts of the woman, and in the flounced skirts they wore.

It so happened that a very great people lived at this time on an island across the sea. The double ax was their symbol. Their women dressed in this manner. And they worshiped the bull. Later a gold cup would be found in another Mycenaean town that showed hunters with bulls. Only then did archaeologists begin to connect Mycenae with this overseas empire.

3

THE AGE OF FABLE

The origin of the Mycenaeans, believed to be the first Greek-speaking people in the land that is now western Greece, is lost in the shadows of prehistory. The first record of them is as Stone Age tribes inhabiting the Danube River Basin in southeastern Europe. They were part of the Aryan people who migrated into Europe from somewhere in central Asia. At one time they were thought to have come from the Caucasus, the mountain range between the Black Sea and the Caspian Sea. They were called Caucasians because of this belief.

The Aryans are not regarded as an individual race of people, but different peoples who spoke a basically common Indo-European language. This is the most important family of languages in the world and is the root of most of today's European languages. Basque, Estonian, Finnish, Hungarian, and Turki are the major exceptions. It is also, in its eastern subdivision, the root of languages spoken in India, the Balkans, Russia, Afghanistan, and Iran, among others.

The language spoken by the future Mycenaeans, now a dead language, was one of the oldest forms of the Indo-European tongue.

We call the people who spoke this language Greeks, and the name is still applied to their descendants, who speak a somewhat different language from their ancestors. However, they are not really Greeks at all. They call themselves Hellenes and their country Hellas. The word "Greek" comes from the Latin *Graeci* and was not applied to the Hellenes until after the days of their greatest glory. "Greek" and

"Greece" are purely foreign words and are not used by the Greeks themselves except when talking with foreigners.

Greece—Hellas—lacks the dry air of Egypt, and its prehistoric material has not survived as well. This makes it difficult to trace the first inhabitants and their migrations into and over the land we now call Greece.

The oldest human remains yet found in Greece were excavated in 1967–1969 at Franchthi cave in the Hermionis area of the Argolid, not too far from the future site of Mycenae. The finds have been dated to the Mesolithic Stone Age, about 8000 B.C. Earlier finds in the Plain of Argos show that these Stone Age people continued to live in the region through the Neolithic, or New Stone Age, which ended around 3000 B.C.

These cave people were probably supplanted by other people coming from the Cyclades Islands of the Aegean Sea during the Early Bronze Age. These people, whoever they were, survived through the Middle (Helladic) Bronze Age, which ended in 1600 B.C. when the Greek-speaking tribes from the Danube region first rose to power in the land we now call Greece.

They may have come earlier, but 1600 B.C. is the first indication we have of them in the Plain of Argos. For a long time there was some question about whether these people spoke Greek or not. The excavation of other Mycenaean areas beyond Mycenae itself settled this question in a dramatic fashion, which will be related later.

In any event, these newcomers called themselves Achaeans (pronounced uh-key-uns). About all that is known of their past is that their Indo-European language indicates that they were part of the Central Asia migration. Pottery finds showed them in the Danube Basin. This was a peculiar type of pottery, fortunately, so it is easy to trace. It was a simple design, either monochrome or with a simple matte decoration. They brought this pottery with them to the Argolid, proving they were the same tribes who had formerly lived in the Danube Basin.

According to Greek mythology, the Achaeans were descendants of Achaeus, the grandson of Hellen, from whom the Greeks take their name of Hellenes. We can suppose that Hellen was a powerful tribal chief of the Danube period and that Achaeus was the leader who brought the Achaean tribes to the Argolid (the Plain of Argos).

The Achaeans were herdsmen and farmers. There is no indication as to why they left the Danube region. They may have exhausted the soil and moved on to better land. They may have been pushed out by tribes that outnumbered them. They were such ferocious fighters after they came to Greece that it is hard to think of them as being dispossessed, except by superior numbers.

The Achaeans did not remain herdsmen and farmers long. Beginning about 1600 B.C., they suddenly began to expand. They moved into the communities first settled by the people they dispossessed. Archaelogical digs in Lerna, Asine, Argos, and Tiryns, in addition to Mycenae, show that Stone Age people had settlements in these places on the Plain of Argos that were taken over by the Greek-speaking invaders.

Evidently these early Greeks had been a landlocked people. When they reached the Plain of Argos, they came into contact with the sea and with traders from such far-off places as Phoenicia, Egypt, Crete, and the Cyclades Islands of the Aegean Sea.

So, around 1600 B.C., the Achaeans began abandoning their mud huts, moved to rocky prominences, and rolled huge rocks into giant walls to create awesome citadels. Two of these grew bigger and more important than the others. One was Tiryns, the legendary home of Heracles, whose mighty exploits are celebrated in Greek mythology.

Tiryns was built on a long, low hill close to the shore of the Bay of Argos. It is about 1,000 feet long and about 400 feet wide. It juts suddenly above the level plain that surrounds it. In prehistoric time it was an island in the bay, but the water receded, leaving a marshy land around the former island. This dried up and was solid ground by the time the first Stone Age people came to the Argolid.

The Tiryns hill, excavations show, was inhabited by people from early in the Neolithic period. Its height made it an easy place to defend. Attackers had to climb steep slopes in the face of stones, clubs, and spears hurled down upon them by the defenders.

When Schliemann came to Mycenae he visited Tiryns, which is only

The rocks used within the walls of Tiryns were so huge that later Greeks thought that giants had built the great citadel.

nine kilometers from Mycenae. Earlier two men had dug there for a short time, but finding nothing of value, they had abandoned the site. Schliemann, taking a few days off from Mycenae, brought in some diggers in August 1876. They uncovered enough dirt to expose some of the huge rocks that make up the walls. But then work at Mycenae reached an exciting stage, and Schliemann abandoned Tiryns to devote his full attention to Mycenae.

His second excavation at Tiryns, made almost ten years later, showed that the citadel was built before Mycenae. The construction is rougher, the rocks more in a natural state. The stones were also larger than those used in Mycenae. Pausanias, who visited the citadel in the second century B.C., said it would have taken two mules to pull one of them into place.

But although Tiryns was the older, Mycenae was the more powerful. This may have been because of its inland position guarding trade routes. Or it may have been because the kings of Mycenae were more able leaders and warriors. At no time in ancient Greece was the country united under a single leader. Each city-state was independent generally, although one might exercise control over a neighboring city or two for a short time.

Although Mycenae was the last of the major cities to be built in the Plain of Argos, its later position of power has caused the entire region to be called Mycenaean. So when we speak of Mycenae, we mean the city or citadel located between Mount Prophet Elias and Mount Zara. But Mycenaean means the entire culture of the Plain of Argos and all its cities and people from 1600 B.C. to 1100 B.C.

At first archaeologists believed that the Mycenaeans did not know writing. Later they found some clay tablets, but these were not deciphered until the 1950's. Unfortunately, the tablets proved to be stores' inventories only. So there are no written records to tell us who the people were who built these cities. There are many myths, often confusing and sometimes in conflict with each other. However, here is the mythological record of the founding of the three greatest Mycenaean cities:

Argos was the oldest. Its name comes from the Pelasgic word for "plain." The Pelasgi were the prehistoric people who inhabited the region before the coming of the Greek-speaking people from the Danube region.

Schliemann, quoting from Pausanias, says:

> On account of its great fertility and remarkable situation on the noble plain [it is about midway between Mycenae and Nauplia on the coast], Argos was the natural central point for the social and political development of the land. . . . Here, as the legend tells, Phoroneus, son of Inarchos and the Nymph Meleia, with his wife Niobe, first gathered the hitherto scattered inhabitants into a community, and founded a town.

The town was renamed for himself by Argos, grandson of Phoroneus. Five kings ruled in Argos before Abas became father of twin sons,

Acrisius and Proetus. The brothers quarreled, and Proetus fled. Later Proetus returned and captured Tiryns. Apparently Tiryns was almost as old as Argos, but it was not the cyclopean citadel it became, for we are told it was Proetus who had the great walls built. Pausanias, Apollodorus, and Strabo all agree that Proetus sent to Sicily for seven Cyclopes, the giant one-eyed men of Greek mythology, to build the walls for him.

Later, the same seven built other walls, including Mycenae, which caused the playwright Euripides to call the Argolid the "cyclopean land."

The two brothers continued to fight. Since all their followers were kin, after one battle the dead were buried together in one giant grave under a single monument for the heroes of both sides.

Acrisius was told in an oracle that he would be slain by his daughter's son. To prevent this, he imprisoned Danaë, his daughter, in a bronze chamber. But Zeus, king of gods, fell in love with Danaë and visited her in a shower of gold. When the child was born, Acrisius—recalling the prophecy—put Danaë and her god-sired son in a box and cast them into the Ionian Sea.

In the manner of good legends, mother and son survived. They landed on an island where the son, Perseus, grew to manhood. Then the local king fell in love with Danaë. Fearing that Perseus might object, the king sent the young man to obtain the head of the gorgon Medusa. Medusa had snakes for hair and eyes that could turn a man to stone.

Perseus defeated the gorgon by using his burnished shield as a mirror. Guided by the reflection of Medusa in the shield, he avoided being turned to stone as he attacked and cut off her head. Perseus then rescued and married Andromeda, daughter of the king of Ethiopia, and returned with the head of Medusa to turn to stone the king who had sent him on the perilous journey.

Perseus, with his mother and wife, returned to Argos, where he accidentally killed his grandfather Acrisius while practicing throwing the discus.

This made Perseus king of Argos, but in his grief he refused the throne. Instead, he exchanged thrones with Megapenthes, son of Proetus, who had succeeded his father as king of Tiryns. It was while he was king of Tiryns that Perseus brought back the Cyclopes to build walls at Mycenae like those of Tiryns.

The time of all this is sunk in myths, but Proetus is believed to be a real person who lived around 1400 B.C.

Perseus was succeeded by his son Electryon, whose daughter Alcmene was the mother of Heracles, the strongman. Electryon abdicated in favor of Amphitryon, grandson of Perseus. Amphitryon was driven out by his uncle Sthenelus. Sthenelus was the son-in-law of Pelops, who came from Asia Minor and was so famous that the entire peninsula is still called Peloponnesus in his honor.

Excavation work is still going on at Tiryns. This shows a "dig" in the lower citadel portion of the great ruins in 1978.

Although Alcmene was married to Amphitryon, Heracles' real father—so the legends say—was Zeus, king of the gods. It was the intention of Zeus that his son should rule Argos and Mycenae. But Hera—Zeus's wife—obtained the throne for Eurystheus, who was also king of Mycenae. Then, through Hera's help, Eurystheus tricked Heracles into becoming his servant.

Heracles had to earn his freedom by performing twelve enormously difficult labors: (1) slaying the Nemean lion; (2) killing the nine-headed Lerna hydra (a dragon); (3) capturing the Erymanthian boar; (4) capturing the hind of Arcadia; (5) killing the terrible man-eating Stymphalian birds; (6) cleaning the Augean stables; (7) capturing the Cretan bull; (8) capturing the man-eating mares of Diomedes; (9) stealing the belt of the Amazon queen (Hippolyte); (10) capturing the red cattle of Geryon; (11) obtaining the golden apples of the Hesperides; and (12) capturing Cerberus, the watchdog of Hell.

After gaining his freedom by performing the twelve labors, Heracles fought a war with his enemy and captured Tiryns. He ruled there for a number of years and then wandered off on new adventures. These included sailing with Jason and the Argonauts to steal the Golden Fleece, and sacking Troy VI because King Priam's father cheated him out of some horses.

The Mycenaean legends now shift from the descendants of Perseus to those of Pelops. Pelops was king of Phrygia, a land north of Troy in Asia Minor. His two sons, Atreus and Thyestes, killed their stepbrother and were banished, coming to Mycenae. In time Atreus married and had two sons, Agamemnon and Menelaus, and became king of Mycenae.

Then Thyestes seduced the wife of his brother, starting a feud between them that would lead to the bloody tragedies recounted by Aeschylus in his famous trilogy, the *Oresteia*. This story, if grounded in truth, may be one of the reasons for the mysterious downfall of Mycenae after the Trojan War.

Thyestes had raised as his own son a child born to Atreus before he left Phrygia. He now cunningly sent this boy to murder his real father, Atreus. This was done for revenge after Atreus had banished Thyestes from Mycenae. Atreus, surprised by the attack, killed the boy. Only then did he learn that he had killed his own son.

Blood vengeance was a family duty in the days of Homer's Greeks. It was absolutely necessary that every violent death be avenged. This was true even within the family itself. If an outsider killed a member of a family, then the family had no recourse but to seek revenge. If it happened within the family, then the family, regardless of its feeling toward the killer, had to take action.

The family, of course, could decide upon what action to take. It did not always demand the blood of the killer. When Atreus and Thyestes killed their stepbrother, their family merely banished them from Phrygia. It depended upon the aggrieved. If the father or another brother had demanded the blood of Atreus and Thyestes and taken it himself, no one would have censured him.

Now Atreus, hating his brother, both because of the seduction of his wife, and the death of the boy, planned a terrible revenge. Atreus had the sons of Thyestes seized and secretly murdered. He then invited Thyestes to a feast at which they would settle their differences and be friendly brothers again. The unsuspecting man came to the feast. After the meal, Atreus—terrible in his vengeance—arose and informed Thyestes that the meat he had eaten was the flesh of his own sons.

Thyestes jumped to his feet and screamed curses upon the House of Atreus and all its descendants. The curse on the House of Atreus took a long time to come to fruit, but it was terrible when it did. As the first step toward Thyestes' vengeance, an unsuspecting Atreus married Thyestes' daughter, agreeing to raise her son. What Atreus did not know was that this boy, Aegisthus, was really the son of Thyestes. In time he would be the instrument of his father's revenge against the House of Atreus.

This revenge was still far in the future when Atreus took the boy to live with his own sons, Agamemnon and Menelaus, in the mighty city of Mycenae.

Under Atreus, Mycenae became even more powerful and wealthier. Of course, it had always been a rich city. The treasures of the shaft graves, found by Schliemann, proved this. But the kings buried in these graves lived two or three hundred years before Atreus, and they do not seem to fit any of the legendary heroes of the myths.

Since this treasure is the richest ever found up to the opening of King Tutankhamen's tomb in Egypt in 1922, the big mystery is: Where did this gold come from? And what did Mycenae do to earn it? This could very well tie in with the mystery of who taught the Mycenaeans how to change from farmers and herdsmen to masters of great citadels in so short a time.

For a while, investigators thought that the teachers of Mycenae may have been the Carians, a seafaring people who came from the islands of the Aegean Sea and settled in Asia Minor. This does not seem reasonable. The Carians were pirates of the worst order. They would have been more likely to steal the Mycenaean cattle and murder the settlers than to aid them.

Gradually evidence built up as to the identity of Mycenae's teachers. The ring Stamatakis found with its bare-breasted women and the double ax was one clue.

Another clue came in Schliemann's later excavations at Tiryns. He originally dug there for a short time in 1876, but came back in 1884 for more serious work. In uncovering the palace walls, a number of remarkable wall paintings were found. They were done in fresco—that is, special colors were applied to wet wall plaster so the colors sank into the plaster. This produced a vivid long-lasting color that survived the years.

The most remarkable painting found was a fragment that showed a charging bull. The center portion was missing, so that it was not easy to determine all that was happening in the picture. But a portion of a man was at the top of the picture. One bent leg rested on the back of the running bull. The other leg was extended straight out behind him. One hand seemed to be reaching forward to touch the bull's horns. He appeared to be wearing only a short garment around his hips, something like modern shorts. And there were bands around the leg just below the knee and again at the ankles.

The painting had a blue background. The bull was painted in yellow with red spots, the man's body in red. It was masterfully done, and there was quite a learned argument about what it meant. Schliemann, ever ready to explain everything by a quotation from Homer, thought it was an acrobat jumping to a bull's back, as Homer described similar actions with horses.

Another group called attention to a coin found in Sicily that showed a bull-headed river god with a man on its back.

Then, in 1889, M. Tsountas, of the Greek Archaelogical Society, dug up two extraordinary golden cups while excavating at Vaphio near Sparta. Carl Schuchhardt (in *Schliemann's Excavations*, published in 1891) quotes a description of the cups by Dr. Paul Wolters:

> They unquestionably give us scenes from everyday life, and represent the capture of half-wild bulls. On one cup we see a palm tree under one of the handles, then further on to the right a bull rushes furiously to the left. He has caught a man on his powerful horns, and throws him headlong to the earth. By the side of the bull another man is falling to the ground. . . . The peculiar costume now becomes clear. The men have long hair, and are naked except for a thick projecting girdle, from which hangs a little apron before and behind. Further, they wear shoes with slightly turned-up points, which are tied half-way up the calf by horizontal thongs.
>
> The whole scene reminds us vividly of the wall-painting at Tiryns [the bull]. Not only the general character of the scene, but the strong build of the bull and the costume of the men, find here their closest parallel.

The cup described, which is now in the Athens museum, showed another bull just back of the one killing the man described by Dr. Wolters. This bull is entangled in a huge net used for his capture. Just behind him is another bull fleeing the scene.

The second Vaphio cup shows captured bulls. It is as beautifully executed as its mate, but does not have such dramatic action.

It was not recognized immediately, but the workmanship and design were pure Cretan. As time went by, this and other evidence turned archaelogical thought more and more toward the island of Crete. There had been a very powerful nation on Crete at the time the Mycenaeans were turning from farmers to barons with great castles.

The greatness of the Cretans and their association with the early Greeks were well founded in both legend and history. Schliemann, again relying entirely upon Homer, had never associated the sea people of Crete with Mycenae's rise to power. In the *Iliad* Crete, "the island of the wine-dark sea," was not overly important but did supply some fighting men to support Agamemnon in the attack on Troy.

However, the legend of Theseus definitely ties Greece to Crete, and suggests a tie with Mycenae. Theseus was the great hero of the Athenians and only second to Heracles as the greatest of the legendary heroes of all Greece. The Mycenaean finds had not been made in the region of the Acropolis of Athens at the time of Schliemann, and he did not realize the tie between Athens and Mycenae. So he never considered the Theseus legends in trying to puzzle out the origin of the Mycenaeans' rise to wealth and glory.

Theseus was the son of King Aegeus of Athens, which was then a vassal state of King Minos of Crete. Each year the Athenians were forced to send a shipload of young men and women to Knossus, capital of Crete, to feed the horrible Minotaur. The Minotaur was a monstrous man with the head of giant bull.

According to legend, Minos refused to sacrifice a prize bull to Poseidon, god of the sea. In revenge, Poseidon caused Minos' queen to fall in love with the bull. The queen prevailed upon Daedalus, a Greek genius employed by Minos, to build her an artificial cow in which she could hide to make love to the bull. This he did, and the secret was revealed when the Minotaur was born. Minos then had Daedalus build the Labyrinth, a confusing maze of corridors under the palace, to hide the bull-headed monster man.

Minos then learned that Daedalus had been responsible for bringing the queen and the bull together. He imprisoned the Greek and his son, Icarus, in the labyrinth. Daedalus made wings by fastening feathers with wax to his and his son's arms. They flew away, but Icarus flew too near the sun. His wings melted, and he plunged to his death in the sea.

Another legend ties this escape to the invention of sail. Before this time all boats were rowed. Daedalus made the first sails to move his boat faster than Minos' sailors could row.

The underground corridors of the Minoan palace at Knossus on the island of Crete gave rise to the legend of the Labyrinth.

In any event, Minos' son was killed while visiting in Athens. The angry sea-king conquered Athens and required the city to furnish seven young men and seven young women to feed the Minotaur. Some accounts say this was done annually. Some say it was every three years.

Then Theseus had himself included in the human tribute. He planned to kill the Minotaur and free Athens from the terrible tribute. The boat carrying the human sacrifices to the bull-monster traditionally carried black sails, a symbol of mourning. Theseus told King Aegeus that if he was successful in killing the Minotaur, the boat would return with white sails. In this way the glad news would reach Greece as soon as the boat cleared the horizon.

Theseus had a stroke of luck upon arriving in Knossus. Ariadne, lovely daughter of Minos, fell in love with the brave and handsome Greek hero. Ariadne told Theseus that the Labyrinth was such a complicated maze that he could never find his way out, even if he did kill the Minotaur. She gave him a ball of string to unwind as he went in. Then he could follow it back later.

Theseus had no weapons. He penetrated to the heart of the Labyrinth and fought the monstrous bull-headed giant with his bare hands. This struggle is often depicted in ancient art as a heroic wrestling match between the two.

Theseus killed the monster and escaped with his ship and the other human sacrifices brought from Greece. He was so overjoyed that he forgot to change the sail. Aegeus, watching from the cliff at Cape Sunion below Athens, saw the black sail. In despair at the supposed death of his beloved son, the king threw himself into the sea. Forever after, the waters have been called the Aegean Sea in his honor.

Those who see fact behind legends and myth believe that this legend is rooted in a distorted account of a Greek raid on Knossus. Another story places Theseus in the time of Atreus of Mycenae. Theseus fell in love with a ten-year-old girl of Sparta who was so beautiful it was said she must be Aphrodite, goddess of beauty, reborn on earth. This girl was Helen. Theseus had her kidnapped, but had to give her back when her vengeful brothers came seeking her. She in turn grew up to marry Menelaus, brother of King Agamemnon of Mycenae. She then ran away with Prince Paris of Troy, thereby becoming the famous Helen of Troy who caused the Trojan War celebrated in the *Iliad*.

In addition to the myths, the Greek historians Thucydides and Herodotus wrote of the fame of King Minos. Schliemann studied these historians as he had Homer and Pausanias. What he read drew him to Crete.

4

THE BULL MEN OF CRETE

Crete is the fourth-largest island in the Mediterranean and forms the border between the Mediterranean Sea and the Aegean Sea. It is about 200 miles north of the African coast and roughly 100 miles southeast of the Greek Peloponnesus. The island is 160 miles in length, east to west, and from 6 to 35 miles wide. It appears to have been inhabited by Neolithic (New Stone Age) people as far back as 3000 B.C.

According to Greek mythology, Cronus was king of the gods. In order to prevent any chance of his being displaced by his sons, Cronus devoured them all. Then, when Zeus was about to be born, his mother Rhea fled to Crete, where Zeus was born in the cave of Dicte on Mount Ida. Then Rhea substituted a stone, which she told Cronus was the child, and the god ate the stone.

Zeus grew up in the Mount Ida area, nourished by milk and honey supplied by a nymph. In time Zeus fell in love with Europa, a girl in Phoenicia. He appeared to her as a giant bull rising out of the sea. Taking her on his back, Zeus brought her back to Crete. The continent of Europe takes its name from Europa. The child born of this marriage became Minos I, king of Crete.

Zeus went on to Olympus, where he overthrew his cruel father and became king of the gods himself. However, he never forgot his son on Crete. Every nine years he would return to the Cave of Dicte to present laws and to ask Minos to account for all he had done in the past nine years.

Minos is recalled as a great lawgiver and the father of his people. When he died, he was honored by being made a judge of the dead in Hades.

Apparently Minos became the name of a dynasty of kings, in the same manner that Egyptian rulers were all called pharaoh. The greatest of the Minoan kings was Minos II, the grandson of Minos I. He was the tyrant king of the Theseus legend.

Enraged because Daedalus escaped his vengeance, Minos pursued the inventor to Sicily. The king of Sicily was reluctant to surrender the famous man, but feared to oppose Minos. So Daedalus disguised himself. Minos was even more crafty. He knew Daedalus could not resist a puzzle. So he challenged the men to find a way to thread a string through a spiral seashell.

One man in the group leaped to the challenge. He harnessed an ant to carry one end of the thread and set it to crawl through the spiral. Minos knew then that he had found the fugitive. He killed Daedalus and then was killed himself by two Sicilian princesses.

However, Minos was historical as well as legendary. Thucydides, the Greek historian, says that Minos was the first king to have a navy. The time of Minos II is not known, but it apparently is at the beginning of the so-called palace-building era, starting around 2000 B.C. At this time the Cretans, who originally came from Asia, were trying to build up trade with the Cyclades islands to the north as well as with the Greek mainland. The Cyclades swarmed with pirates, and Minos II built his navy to bring them under control. This he did, destroying the pirates and taking over their islands. This navy was so powerful that he did not bother to build walls around his palaces and towns, but relied on the power of his "wooden walls"—his ships.

The rise of the Minoan civilization—named for Minos—in Crete coincided with the coming of the first Greek-speaking people to the Peloponnesus and the beginning of Mycenae's startling change. As this fact became more and more apparent to archaeologists, Schliemann's interest in Crete was aroused.

In 1883 he heard that a Greek named Minos Kalokairinos, who lived in Crete, had dug in a hill five kilometers outside of Candia (Heraklion) in Crete and had found some ancient walls. The site was the reputed location of Knossus, the capital of King Minos. Schliemann made some inquiries about continuing the work there, but Crete was then controlled by the Turks, and he was told that he was not welcome.

He went back to Greece to do his famous excavations at Tiryns, following up the brief work he had done there while working at Mycenae. Then, in 1889, he went back to Crete. After considerable negotiation with a Turk who claimed to own the hill, Schliemann agreed to buy the location for 50,000 French francs. In addition he agreed to pay for 2,500 olive trees that would be destroyed in the excavations. Ever the canny businessman, Schliemann personally went to the location and counted the trees to ensure that he was not being defrauded. He found only 888 trees. In a rage at the deception, he broke off the negotiations.

It was well that he did, for the Turk owned only one third of the land. Starting anew with the other two owners, Schliemann finally made a new deal, but the owner of the first third, enraged at Schliemann for calling him a crook over the olive-tree deal, flatly refused to have any more dealings with the German. Schliemann, ever impatient when crossed, withdrew and returned to Greece. This impatience robbed him of making another great discovery equal to those at Troy and Mycenae.

The man who would finally reveal the true greatness of the Minoan empire was an Englishman, Sir Arthur John Evans. No archaeologist before or since ever made himself so much a part of a site as Evans did at Knossus. From 1899 until his death in England in 1941, he was "Mr. Knossus." Using his own money, he restored large sections of the Minoan ruins. When he discovered famed frescoes and wall paintings, he had them removed, as Schliemann and others had done at Tiryns. But unlike the others, he then called in a painter and had a duplicate copy made to put back in place of the original, which went to the Heraklion museum. It is said that he spent over a million dollars of his own money—at a time when a million was worth many times what it is today—to restore sections of the ancient city he had grown to love so dearly.

Actually when Evans first came to Crete, he was not interested in excavating buildings at all. He was searching for carved seals for a collection he had been making. He became fascinated with the site, and its spell completely absorbed him.

He was extremely fortunate in two respects. His father was rich and was also an amateur archaeologist. He fully supported his son's work as long as he lived, and left him a generous inheritance that permitted Evans to carry on the work up to the opening of World War II in 1939.

Evans was one of those fortunate people who never had to work for a living, although his extravagance in archaeology often left him tight for money. He traveled widely, following his father in his love of archaeology and numismatics. John Evans, the father, had assembled one of the world's greatest collections of ancient coins.

In 1884 Evans became curator of the Ashmolean Museum at Oxford University. He had fought hard against continuing frustrations to get the position, which was one of honor rather than profit. He then plunged into a long and bitter fight to expand the museum. In those times, museum directors were expected to study and keep up with what was developing in their specialty. Thus their museum work was arranged to take up only six months of the year. This permitted Evans to travel and continue his own collecting.

He met Schliemann in Athens and was greatly impressed by the treasures of Troy and Mycenae. However, his own interest was still in collecting ancient seals. From this he became interested in ancient writing and was drawn to markings on Mycenaean seals. Later he bought some Mycenaean seals from a dealer in Athens and was surprised to learn that they had been found in Crete.

This led him, like Schliemann several years earlier, to the huge mound at Knossus. He decided to dig there, but was put off by internal trouble. Crete was still under Turkish control, and troubles broke out between the Muslim and Christian elements. This brought Greece and Turkey into conflict, ending with a group of major European nations taking over the island to keep the peace. They then in effect gave the island to Greece, by placing it under King George I of Greece.

In the meantime, Evans had bought the entire Knossus hill. All he needed was government permission to excavate. This King George was delighted to give. No restrictions were placed on the archaeologist, other than that the finds—except duplicates—would go to the Heraklion museum. This left Evans more fortunate than other archaeologists. He owned the land. He could do whatever he wanted to do. He could tear down walls, dig where he chose, work when he wished, and stay as long as necessary without worrying about getting his official permission renewed.

His success was stunning. Some archaeologists dig for weeks and months before finding anything of value. Evans began work on March 23, 1899. On the second day his diggers had uncovered enough of a wall to disclose part of a fresco that looked promising. On the fourth day they uncovered a drain filled with pottery and enough walls to indicate there might have been something to the myth of the Labyrinth. The walls seemed to create a genuine maze. Two days later they uncovered the top portions of huge jars, called *pithoi*, in which the ancient people stored oil and grain.

The find on April 5, just thirteen days after the digging began, was so important that Evans jubilantly wrote in his journal that the Minoan (as he later termed the Cretan civilization, taking the name from King Minos) would prove to be greater than anything previously discovered in the Aegean area.

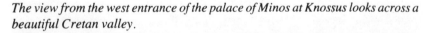

The view from the west entrance of the palace of Minos at Knossus looks across a beautiful Cretan valley.

The find was a piece of a large, life-size fresco painting showing what he thought was a woman holding a funnel-shaped jar. Later this was proved to be a man. The figure had the tight pinched-in waist and the short apron garments worn by the bull catchers in the famous Vaphio cups found near Sparta in Greece. Here was another link between Mycenae and Crete. Since Crete was several hundred years the older, it was becoming more and more apparent that it was the Minoans from Knossus on Crete who had been the teachers of the Mycenaeans.

This growing belief was strengthened when an ivory statue of a Cretan snake goddess was found. She had the same bare breasts and the flounced skirt of the goddess and the priestesses on the signet ring Stamatakis had found at Mycenae.

At first it was believed that only the priestesses dressed in this fashion. The bare breasts would be suitable for the hot Cretan climate, but the flounced, bell-bottomed skirt would be uncomfortably hot. Then Evans uncovered a series of small paintings that showed groups of women sitting around, obviously gossiping. They were all dressed in the same manner.

Discoveries tumbled over each other as the digging continued. Many of them strengthened the evidence of the strong ties between Mycenae and Crete. As more walls were uncovered, the suggestion of a maze that could have given birth to the myth of the Labyrinth became more certain. As for the legendary Minotaur that inhabited the maze in the Greek legend of Theseus, a giant bull's head in plaster was found on one wall.

Even more to the point, Crete is in the earthquake belt of the Mediterranean. Some of the layers of Knossus showed evidence of considerable earthquake damage. Evans wrote that he was working in his home, the Villa Ariadne, near the ruins, when a strong earthquake hit. The tremor lasted for one and a quarter minutes, during which time the walls shook and the ground heaved. Evans said that the sound of the moving earth under the hill of Knossus sounded like the muffled bellow of a giant bull.

In this we can see the possible origin of the myth that a monster bull lived in a maze in the depths of the hill. There is no question that the bull was important in the lives of the Minoan people of Crete. It is believed that cattle always inhabited Crete, but were not brought there by the

Neolithic people who floated over on log rafts or in dugout canoes. Probably during the Ice Age, when so much water was locked up in glaciers, the level of the sea was lower, and a land bridge existed between Crete and one of the mainlands.

It was as a bull that Zeus brought Minos' mother Europa to Crete. Bulls' heads decorated the palace. Projections representing bulls' horns were placed around the court of the palace. There have even been suggestions that Minos wore a bull mask, and it was this that gave rise to the legend of the Minotaur. The Theseus legend that the human tribute from Athens fed the bull monster is another indication of the importance of the bull in the Minoan culture. Yet for all this emphasis upon the bull as some kind of symbol, he does not seem to have been worshiped, as Egyptians revered Apis, their sacred bull-god.

In fact, one of the most remarkable of all the frescoes discovered in the Knossus palace ruins points to the bull as an object of sport.

This is the famous "bull-leaper" fresco found in the House of the Olive Spout during the second year of Evans' excavation. The original was carefully removed and placed in the Heraklion Museum. A duplicate was painted and placed in the restored throne room at the ruins.

The picture shows a charging bull. A girl clad only in a waist girdle is

The famous "bull-leaper" fresco found by Evans in the ruins of Knossus. It is now in the museum at Heraklion.

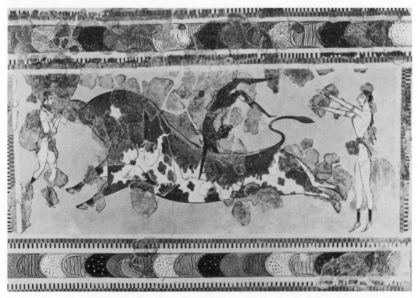

holding the bull's horns in front. A man has somersaulted to the bull's back. His hands are forking the animal and his head is to the rear. His legs are swinging backward toward the bull's tail. Another woman stands behind the bull's hind hooves. Her hands are upraised as if to catch the acrobatic man as he leaps off the bull's back. Like the first woman, the other two figures are nude except for the short apron about their waists and shoes or stocking that come high up the ankles. The women wear bracelets around their wrists and upper arms. In the stylized tradition of Minoan painting, the man's body is a dark red, and the women are painted in white.

The painting is a masterpiece, but from an archaelogical standpoint it ties the Mycenaean world even more tightly to Minoan Crete. Evans immediately recognized the painting as similar to the fresco Schliemann had uncovered in Tiryns. This is the one that showed the charging bull with a red-bodied man apparently kneeling on the animal's back.

By itself the Tiryns painting was just a curiosity. Now the bull-leaper fresco of Knossus proved that this sport—if sport it proves to be—was widespread. This was verified by the discovery of rings, seals, and other representations of the bull jumpers. Two small ivory carvings of leaping men have been found, suggesting that they were originally suspended on gold wires over a small statue of a bull.

The various representations show very clearly what happened. The bull leaper approached the charging bull from directly in front. He grasped the animal's horns and swung himself up in a somersault to straddle the bull's back. Then another flip in the air brought him to a landing behind the animal.

All the pictures show men doing the actual leaping, although the position of the woman grasping the bull's horns in some of the frescoes indicates that women also took part in the leaping.

But although *what* happened is clear enough, *why* it happened is still lost among the many remaining mysteries of Mycenae and Knossus.

Bull leaping does not appear to have a religious significance. More probably, it was a sport, as bull fighting is in some countries today. However, it is not clear if the bull leapers were volunteers, professional athletes, or condemned people like most of the gladiators of Rome. In her fictional account of the Theseus legend, *The King Must Die*, novelist Mary Renault created a fanciful picture of the Athenian human tribute trained for the dangerous sport of bull leaping.

All we have for evidence in any case are the pictures themselves. The action of a charging bull is well known from observations of modern bull fighting. A bull hooks to the left and follows movements. This is the reason for the cape, which the matador uses to distract the bull and draw the horns away from him.

It is nearly impossible for a person to meet a charging bull head-on, grasp its horns and flip over its back. Some observers have suggested that the bull was trained and knew his role in the play. The frescoes found both in Knossus and Tiryns show the bull at full gallop. Although the bull's head is tucked, it is not lowered in a hooking position such as we see in a modern bullfight. The horns are very long and extend directly forward, which suggests that they were trained to grow forward for easier grasping. This further suggests that the bull may have been especially bred for the games.

They may have been trained to run on command and to hold a steady course. If they hooked like modern bulls, bull leaping would have been suicidal.

The bull leapers themselves had to have been superb athletes. They were probably professionals, selected as children and trained for this most dangerous of sports. Even if the bull had been bred and trained to be cooperative, it was still dangerous to face the running animal and grab the sharply pointed horns. The frescoes show that the horns were not blunted.

No real bullring has been found. There may have been one outside the palace or the games may have been held in the central court.

Knossus, as uncovered by Evans, was not a city. It was only the sprawling palace of the kings. The actual city was spread out from below the palace hill to the sea five kilometers away. There is no evidence to show how the people lived, but life in the palace must have been pleasant. The buildings were placed to catch the cool breezes of morning and evening. There were clever drainage systems to carry away the rain and a very good piped water supply. Beautiful paintings on the walls, awesome staircases, and light wells to provide interior illumination gave the palace an airy, pleasant-to-live-in aspect missing in the gloomy corridors of the great castles of Europe. As one wanders through the restored areas today, there is the distinct feeling that the entire labyrinth of rooms was designed for comfort.

The fact that there were no walls around the town showed that this was a peaceful island and that the people as a whole were content.

The great navy built by Minos I suppressed piracy in the Cyclades islands, and the trading ships of the Minoans sailed to far ports. They may even have traded with Egypt. Figures in wall pictures found there were identified as Keftiu in Egyptian, but closely resemble the wasp-waisted men we find in the wall pictures of Knossus.

It would appear then that the Mycenaeans first made contact with the Cretans through trading ships from Knossus that put in to the Gulf of Argos. The first contact would have been made through Tiryns, which was then nearer the sea than it is today. From these traders the My-cenaeans learned of a better life than their own hard struggle. The Greeks have always been extremely intelligent as a race, and they easily and quickly absorbed the Minoan culture.

The great period of Mycenaean building came around 1600 B.C., but the first contact with the men of Minos must have started a hundred years before. We can see a modern parallel to this in the history of Cambodia. At the beginning of the Christian era, highly civilized Hindus from India settled in Fu-nan in what is now south Cambodia. Here they found tribes of natives so savage they had not yet learned to wear clothing. Savage or not, these natives were intelligent. It only took them two hundred years to absorb the culture of their captors and to displace them as the ruling class. They went on from there to build the great Kambujan empire, climaxing in the amazing city of Angkor with its famous temple, Angkor Wat, which is still one of the wonders of the modern world.

Although the rise of Mycenae is not as well documented, it appears to have followed along the same groove. There is no evidence that the Minoans ever exercised an overlordship over the Greeks, but the Greeks of Mycenae did ape the culture and knowledge of the Minoans without losing their own identity. The art and the sciences, such as they were,

were copied, but the Greeks clung to their own costumes and developed their own building style. The difference in clothing was due to a harsher climate, and the great castles were necessary not only to protect them from foreign foes, but to protect them from each other. Greece in olden times was never a unified country, and the city-states warred almost constantly with one another. Then, if there was no enemy without, the belligerent Greek royal families fought among themselves. Neither history nor legend show the Greeks as peace-loving people.

The curious thing about the early Mycenaeans is that, as early as 1600 B.C., the date assigned to the shaft graves where Schliemann found the Mycenaean treasure, they had great wealth. The golden masks, rings, jewelry, cups, inlaid daggers, and swords were one of the largest archaeological gold hoards found outside Egypt. The Mycenaeans must have had plenty more to be able to bury it with their kings. Where did it come from?

The gold certainly did not come from Greece itself. It could have come from other countries to Mycenae either through plundering or through extensive trade. We have no evidence of either. Plunder and piracy do not seem logical. The great navy of Minos kept order in the Aegean Sea regions. Also, the Greeks at that time were not a seafaring people. They came from landlocked Europe, and the sea was new to them. The ancient mariners who went down to the sea in the fragile ships of the time were a race apart from ordinary men.

Later, the Greeks did develop into sailors. We see hints of this in the account of Jason and the Argonauts sailing up through the Hellespont to the Black Sea. The legend that they brought back the Golden Fleece is interpreted by some as an account—distorted by myths—of the Greeks' first trading expedition to a faraway land. But if the Mycenaeans' wealth was based upon trade, what did they trade? One writer suggested that they might have hired themselves out as mercenary soldiers. But this is a guess. The source of the gold of Mycenae is still an unsolved mystery. One thing now seems certain, however: in time the Mycenaeans became more powerful than their Minoan teachers and moved into Knossus itself. The sinking of ''lost Atlantis'' may have had something to do with this.

5

THE FALL OF KNOSSUS

Some sixty miles north of Crete is an island called Santorin or Santorini. This is a modern name and comes from a crewman of a Portuguese ship who died there during a voyage. The island is also known by its more ancient name of Thera.

Thera is one of the Cycladic islands that were subdued by Minos I. Like Mycenae, Thera absorbed Minoan culture and in time became very much like a Cretan town.

Then sometime between 1500 B.C. and 1400 B.C.—timing prehistoric events is not exact—the volcanic island of Thera exploded. The disaster seems to have begun with a major eruption followed by earthquakes. Then a break in the crust of the island permitted the ocean to pour into the hot interior of the volcano. The tremendous steam pressure ripped out the center of the island. What had been a fairly round-shaped land became a rim of islands marking the outer edge of the former island.

Today what had been the interior of Thera is now part of the ocean. Ships can sail directly into the former crater. It is a weird experience, for towering volcanic cliffs rise high on the sides of the remaining islands. The tiny white buildings on top gleam brilliantly against the darkness of the cliffs. The largest of the remaining fragments of the original island is called Thera, although the entire group is usually referred to as Santorini.

At the back edge of Thera, at the site of a prehistoric seaport, archaelogists found the remains of the city of Akroteri. It is not as grand as Knossus, nor as awesome as Mycenae, but in its own way Akroteri has made a tremendous contribution to our knowledge of the Minoan-Mycenaean world. Like Pompeii in Italy, Akroteri was covered with volcanic ash. This packed around the walls, holding them intact so they were not leveled like most of those in Knossus. Also, as in Pompeii, the ash acted as a preservative for the wall paintings. This left them in a better state than any of those found in Tiryns or Knossus.

Akroteri was not a palace or a citadel like Knossus, Mycenae, and Tiryns. This was an ordinary city where the non-nobility lived, and we can see in it how the people lived, how they ate, and how their children played.

The town had narrow cobblestone streets. These widened in places to create town squares. Houses, usually two to four stories high, were jammed on each side of the streets. Round pipes molded of clay were sunk under the houses to carry away waste water.

The walls were made of stone, held together by a clay mortar, but the walls were broken at proper points by wooden joists to keep the walls from being too rigid. This was so they would not crack so easily when shaken by the numerous earthquakes caused by the rumbling volcano which had originally given birth to the island.

The lower floor of the house was not decorated. Tools found in them and sometimes the number of doors indicated that they might have been used as shops or for manufacturing, with the family living on the upper floors. Except in one case, all wall paintings were on the upper floor. Some of the houses had basements where magazines of *pithoi*, the huge storage jars, were kept. Traces of flour, barley, almonds, and dried fish were found in them. Others stored olive oil and wine. From some of the wall painting, we can see that the people also farmed and raised sheep, goats, pigs, and some beef. From all indications, they were well fed.

The great interest is in the wide variety of painting. In one we can see soldiers with square shields and the boar's-tusk helmets of both Mycenae and Crete lined up with brandished spears. Another portion looks like naked bodies of the enemy plunging off cliffs into the sea.

An especially beautiful painting shows a naked youth carrying two heavy strings of fish. His body is painted red in the Minoan manner. In another house there is a delightful life-size painting of two young boys boxing. They are nude with a band around their stomachs and their hair is in long braids like that of the Cretans. They appear to be wearing a boxing glove on the right hand, with the left hand bare. On the adjoining wall of the same room there are two beautifully executed antelopes. They are painted with broad heavy brown lines, somewhat resembling Oriental sumi painting.

A different building has the walls of a room covered with blue monkeys swinging around. Another has giant plants that resemble the Egyptian papyrus, from which paper got its start and name.

There is a painting of a priestess holding a burning brazier. She has no resemblance to the priestesses shown in the Mycenae and Knossus work. In another there is a woman who wears the bell-bottom dress of Crete, but unlike the women of Knossus, she wears a blouse. Also her features are much less delicate than those of the women of the land of Minos.

One long murallike strip shows a procession of boats. They seem to be escorting a group of officials. The boat is ornamented with yellow decorations hanging from stays (lines of standing rigging) extending from the top of the mast to the bowsprit and fantail. There is no sail. Rowers are in use, although some of the escort boats have small sails in addition to paddles. The boats do not resemble the low-prowed, high-sterned craft we see on Greek pottery depicting Odysseus. These boats all have pointed and uplifted sterns and bows in the manner of the old Egyptian papyrus boats, although these obviously are of wood.

Since the oarsmen are sitting down and partially hidden by the gunwales, it is not possible to tell how they are dressed. They are naked at least to the waist and their skins are painted red in the Minoan tradition. However, the steersmen standing in the rear of the boat have wasp waists and loin aprons much like the bull leapers of Crete. We can assume that the oarsmen are similarly dressed.

The boxing-boys fresco, painted in reds, greens, and black, was found on a house wall in Akroteri, the prehistoric city on Thera. Although definitely showing Minoan influence, the Therans had a distinctive art style of their own.

Since the passengers wear long robes, it appears that only the working class wears the Cretan miniature loin apron.

A study of Akroteri is fascinating for the insight it gives into the everyday life in Minoan-Mycenaean times, but we have digressed to take in this island for a more important reason. This is the possible light it may shed on the fall of Knossus and the takeover of Crete by Homer's Greeks.

The different layers of ash and pumice that covered Akroteri told vulcanologists a lot about what happened during the eruption. It appears that it began with a small earthquake. This seems to have warned the people to get out of the houses, for a much more devastating quake followed, which knocked down many walls. However, no skeletons or valuable possessions were found in the rubble. This indicates that the people got away before the destruction hit.

Then there was a quiet period. Evidence shows that the people came back and began clearing the streets. Another warning caused them to flee again. This time they did not come back. Water poured into the cracks in the volcano cone, and the blast ripped the island to pieces.

There is no clue to where the people went. If they fled inland, they were destroyed by the exploding island. If they took to boats, then they may have gotten away to another island, or their boats may have been—and probably were—swamped by the falling rock or the raging sea.

The amount of material that fell from the sky was enormous. In many places on Thera the layers of ash and pumice are over a hundred feet thick.

We can get a pretty good idea of what happened at Thera by comparing it to Krakatoa, the island between Java and Sumatra, which exploded in the same manner in 1883. The area that sank at Thera was four times greater than at the Indonesian island, and that one threw pumice for hundreds of miles, causing spectacular sunsets around the world. In addition it caused cataclysmic tidal waves that swept over adjoining islands. The waves reached a crest of fifty feet, and effects of the tidal wave were felt as far away as Cape Horn at the tip of South America, seven thousand miles away.

The town of Thera sits atop a high cliff made of successive layers of volcanic lava and ash. The water in the foreground was land before the giant explosion that almost entirely destroyed the island between 1500 and 1400 B.C.

Excavations have shown that pumice rocks and layers of pumice rained down on Crete, which was only sixty miles from the eruption. Calculating the force of the tidal wave churned up by the underwater explosion, the flooding of Crete would have been devastating. Waves probably crashed over the palace hill at Knossus. The Plain of Argos is twice as far from Thera as Crete, but even so, there should have been considerable flooding in the then marshy lowlands around Tiryns, Nauplia, and Asine, although it is doubtful that it could have reached Mycenae in the hills.

Some historians have pinpointed the destruction of Thera as the event that triggered the downfall of the Minoan civilization. Knossus was still in existence after this time, but it declined rapidly. Some say the volcanic ash may have been so thick that it killed the island's agriculture. More likely it was not damage to the land by ash or tidal flooding that crippled the Minoans, but destruction of their navy and merchant fleet. None of the frail ships of the time could have ridden out the monstrous waves raised by the Thera explosion. Those in the sea would have sunk. Those in harbor or near land would have been smashed against the shore. Since it was the navy that made Crete powerful and prosperous, the loss would have been a blow from which it would have been difficult to recover. We must remember that they would not only have lost the ships, but their trained captains and sailors as well. These would have been impossible to replace.

This would have opened the Minoans to their enemies. It would have lessened their standard of living as trade fell off abruptly. It might also have sapped their morale as their faith in their protective gods lessened.

In any event the power of the sea kings of Crete declined. At the same time, the power of Mycenae increased. Some strange writing found by Evans in the ruins of Knossus indicate that Mycenae took over Knossus and the island of Crete. This, however, was a long time being discovered. Evans, despite years of work, was unable to read the writing. It was not deciphered until the 1950's, when it startled the historical and archaeological world with new evidence of the greatness of the people we call Homer's Greeks.

As for exploding Thera, it may have sparked the decline of the Minoan kings, but it has also fathered another aspect of the great Atlantean controversy.

The idea of a great civilization whose island and culture sank in the sea has intrigued people since the days of Plato in Classical Greece. According to Plato, Solon, the great Athenian lawgiver, visited Egyptian priests in the city of Sais. They told him of a war between Athens and an island kingdom in the Atlantic Ocean. This happened nine thousand years ago, they told him. Atlantic means "of Atlas," the Greek hero who held the world on his shoulders.

The Atlanteans conquered Libya and parts of Italy. Then they made war on Egypt and Greece. But Athens, ''surpassing all others in magnanimity and military skill,'' defeated the invading Atlanteans.

This, the Egyptians told Solon, ensured the blessing of freedom upon the people living within the Pillars of Hercules (that is, the Strait of Gibralter), the Mediterranean world.

Sometime after the defeat, Atlantis was struck by devastating earthquakes and deluges. It sank beneath the sea.

Plato first told this story, which he got from a descendant of Solon, in *Timaeus*. Later he expanded the story in another dialogue, *Critias*. In this dialogue he told of the greatness of Atlantis. It was a round island with a series of circular canals. It had magnificent buildings. The docks were jammed with merchant vessels from all parts of the world. The king's palace was said to have been tremendous and had fountains and baths. Bulls grazed in the land around the temples. The citizens went swordless and hunted the wild bulls, which they sacrificed to Poseidon, god of the sea, catching the blood in cups and spilling it in libations to the gods.

Now this, and other things Plato said of Atlantis, is almost a perfect description of Knossus in the days of its glory. The jammed harbors, the magnificent buildings, the bulls, and even the cups to catch blood at the sacrifices. A number of *rhytons* (drinking horns) for sacrifices have been found. Some were in the shape of a bull's head. There was a hole in the back to put the blood into, and it was poured out of silver-rimmed holes in the model's nostrils.

The ''swordless citizens'' perfectly described the people of Knossus, and the catching of bulls is depicted on the famous Vaphio cups.

These close similarities caused a number of authorities to claim that Plato was describing Crete. However, there are three points that do not agree with Crete. One is the circular shape Plato attributed to Atlantis. The second is that he placed Atlantis beyond the Pillars of Hercules (Gibralter) in the Atlantic Ocean. The third discrepancy is that Crete, although it was probably drenched in the tidal wave from Thera, did not sink into the sea.

In recent years, Dr. A. G. Galanopoulos, a Greek seismologist, wrote a book to prove that Atlantis was really Thera. Almost all the lines in Plato describing Atlantis fit Thera as they did Crete. In addition, Thera was originally a round island, and it certainly did sink into the sea—or at least most of it did.

Plato placed the time as nine thousand years before the age of Solon. Galanopoulos said that this is a mistake that crept into the story as it passed from hand to hand. An extra zero was added, and the true date was nine hundred years. Solon lived from 637 to 559 B.C. If we pick a midpoint in his life, say 510 B.C., and add the nine hundred years suggested by Galanopoulos, we get 1410 B.C. The generally accepted time for the destruction of Thera is around 1500 B.C.; however, carbon dating of organic matter found in the ruins places the destruction at about 1410 B.C. All methods of dating prehistoric events have a large plus/ minus error factor, but all agree that the destruction was somewhere between 1500 and 1400 B.C., and also that the fall of Knossus can be dated at about 1450 B.C. All this ties in neatly with the theory that Thera was the model for Plato's Atlantis.

The only thing that does not coincide with Plato's story is that Plato placed Atlantis, as its name implies, in the Atlantic Ocean "beyond the Pillars of Hercules."

Although there have been many claims and theories, no real trace of a sunken island has been found in the Atlantic that can be identified as the true Atlantis. One theory holds that Plato was only telling a fiction story to illustrate his ideas of what a perfect republic would be like. He based his account upon the legends he had heard about the Minoan world and the destruction of Thera. Another ingenious theory is that the term "Pillars of Hercules" does not refer to Gibraltar at all. Tiryns was the home of Hercules for a number of years, and this theory maintains that the Pillars of Hercules are the walls of the city and that Greeks of the interior referred to Thera as "beyond the place of Hercules," or Tiryns.

What is more likely, the Greeks of 1500 B.C. saw their coast hit by a giant tidal wave and found their skies red with unusual sunsets caused by floating pumice and ash in the air. Rumors from sailors told of a great island sinking in the sea. This island, the Greeks were told, was far, far away. As the story was repeated down the years, it became enlarged and took on the dress of myths that placed it out in the unknown sea. Thus the idea of Lost Atlantis may well have originated in the cataclysm that destroyed Thera.

Just exactly what effect the Thera explosion had upon Knossus is not known. Speculation is that it destroyed the navy and merchant fleet and the Minoan nation went into a decline. According to Evans, the great palace was destroyed by fire and perhaps vandalism and was never repaired. Earlier it was destroyed about 1600 B.C., but rebuilt on a grander scale than ever. After the destruction of around 1450 B.C., it was not rebuilt, although the island itself continued to be inhabited and even played a part in the Trojan War, which some accounts date as about 1270 B.C.

There are hints that the Mycenaean Greeks took over from their Minoan teachers after the destruction of Knossus and the other cities of Crete. Herodotus tells how Cretans of the Minoan city of Praesus recounted a story that, after Crete was destroyed, "other men, and especially the Greeks went and settled there."

There is not even a legend to show that the Mycenaeans fought a war with the Minoans, but there is definite proof through the famous Linear-B tablets, found both in Mycenae and in Knossus, that shows that the Greeks did rule Crete for a period of time. But apparently it was a peaceful takeover. The fact that Evans found evidence of great fires in the ruins of the palace is not a positive indication of war. The palace could have been burned as an aftermath of the great earthquakes that followed the Thera explosion.

In any event, the fortunes of the Mycenaeans rose as those of the Minoans of Crete fell. We can see this in the mighty citadels they built and in the riches they buried with their kings. Also, Mycenae seems to have taken over a lot of the Mediterranean trade formerly carried by the Minoan ships. Mycenaean pottery has been found in the ruins of Tel el Amarna, the ghost city of the heretic king of Egypt, Akhenaten. This strange man reigned from 1375 to 1358 B.C. and was the father-in-law of the famous King Tutankhamen. The presence of Mycenaean pottery in

Tel el Amarna may provide a clue to where the Mycenaean kings got their gold. Egypt was exceptionally rich in gold in this period. In the library of official records found at the site, a king of Mitanni, a country in central Asia Minor, wrote Akhenaten begging for gifts of gold. "Gold is like dust in your country," he wrote.

Although Egypt was undoubtedly the source of Mycenaean gold, it does not seem possible that the Greeks could have sold enough of their pottery, beautiful as it was, to account for the riches Schliemann found in the shaft graves. Also, archaeologists now believe that these graves date back to three hundred years before Akhenaton.

Turning to Homer, we find that the Cretans fought with the Greeks in the Trojan War of 1275 B.C. Homer, in the catalog of ships, says:

> And of the Cretans Idomeneus the famous spearman was leader, even of them that possessed Knossos and Gortys of the great walls, Lyktos and Miletos and chalky Lykastos and Phaistos and Rhytion, established cities all; and of all the others that dwell in Crete of the hundred cities. Of these men was Idomeneus leader. With these followed eighty black ships.

"Crete of the hundred cities," the beautiful land in "the wine-dark sea," certainly does not sound like a devastated, deserted land at this time. Of course, this was about 175 years after the presumed date of Knossus' destruction in 1450 B.C. There are not even legends to tell us what happened during those years.

We do know that Idomeneus, the great spearsman, came to a sad end. After he returned to Crete at the end of the Trojan War, the island was hit by a great plague. The king was blamed and driven out.

At this point Crete drops out of the Mycenaean story, but it was revived in 1952 with the dramatic decipherment of the long mysterious Linear-B writing found in both Mycenae, Pylos, and Crete. In the meantime, Mycenae reached its peak of glory in the Trojan War before its splendor and heroes crumbled, leaving only mammoth walls and ruins as their monuments.

6

THE MYCENAEANS AT TROY

Homer's Greeks reached the peak of their glory at Troy. In the *Iliad* and indirectly in the *Odyssey*, the blind poet sang of epic adventures that have gripped the imagination of men of many nations ever since.

Troy is on the coast of Turkey, a few miles from the mouth of the Dardanelles (the Hellespont), the strait where the Aegean Sea joins the Sea of Marmara to separate Asia and Europe. Its position gave the Trojans command of trade going by water into the Black Sea, and by land into Asia Minor.

Excavations have proved that Troy was actually nine cities, extending from the Stone Age to Roman times. The first habitation was a stone-and-mud town going back to 3000 B.C., more than a thousand years before the rise of Minoan Crete.

The second Troy, built on the ruins of the first in 2500 B.C., was a well-built and important city, arising at the same time that Cheops was building the Great Pyramid in Egypt. When this city was destroyed in 2200 B.C., presumably by war, three other cities were built one after another on the site. Each time the ruins of the preceding city were leveled and the new buildings and walls constructed on the ever-rising hill created by the growing levels of rubble. The fifth of the nine Troys appears to have been destroyed about 1800 B.C.

Up to this point it is not clear where the original Trojans came from. Later Greek myths indicate that they came from the same source as the Mycenaeans, but moved farther north to cross into Asia Minor at the

Bosporus, the strait between the Sea of Marmara and the Black Sea in Russia.

They then migrated into what is now Turkey. Finally a branch under Ilus founded Troy under the name "Ilium." This name is the source of the *Iliad*, the Homeric epic.

This account only partially agrees with archaeology. A study of the pottery and artifacts in Troy I through V show a progression of the same kind of people. They worshiped Asiatic gods and were not Greek. Then there is a break in time and culture. The people of the new Troy VI do appear to have been of Greek origin.

Also the legends now begin to tie Troy and Mycenae together. One tells of the destruction of Troy VI by Heracles of Tiryns. Earlier Zeus gave Tros of Phrygia three immortal horses. These were inherited by Ilus, who passed them on to his son Laomedon, who became king of Troy when Ilus died.

Laomedon asked Zeus for help in strengthening Troy's walls. Zeus sent Poseidon and Apollo to build a stronger wall. When Laomedon refused to pay the two gods for their labor, Poseidon sent a sea monster to ravage the city. An oracle told the king that the monster would depart if the king sacrificed his daughter to it.

Laomedon bewailed his fate. He put out princess Hesione on the beach, but promised the immortal horses to any hero who could save her.

Heracles, on his way to the Black Sea with the Argonauts, heard of this. He stopped and killed the monster in a savage fight, saving Hesione. But once again Laomedon tried to avoid paying his debt. He substituted three ordinary horses. The outraged hero went to Poseidon for help. The god was angry with Heracles for killing his sea beast, but he hated Laomedon more. He broke the walls of Troy with a mighty earthquake. Heracles and his men stormed through. Laomedon was killed and his five sons captured.

Hesione begged Heracles to spare one of the sons so that Troy would not be without a king. He asked her to choose one. She picked Podarces, the youngest. Heracles then asked for a ransom for the boy. All Hesione had to give was her veil, all else was lost in the fighting. Heracles gallantly accepted it. From that time Podarces was called Priam, which means "ransomed."

Priam rebuilt the partially destroyed walls to create Troy VIIa, which archaeologists identify as the Troy of the *Iliad*.

Archaeology supports the basic facts of the legend. Pottery demonstrates that the Troy VI Trojans were of Greek origin. They came from Thrace and were the Ionian branch of the original Greek-speaking people from the Danube basin. The ruins of Troy VI show evidence of destruction by a severe earthquake. The city was definitely rebuilt by Troy VI people, who used part of the Troy VI walls in building Troy VIIa.

In the foreground is a section of the main gate of Troy VI. The gate was not entirely destroyed in the earthquake that ruined Troy VI, and parts were used in constructing the gate of Troy VIIa, the Troy of Homer's Iliad.

And if Heracles was a historical person, as some believe, he could well have led an attack on Troy. It would probably have been a piratical raid.

Then, in Priam's old age, the Mycenaean Greeks caused the Trojan War. Many writers—some of the world's greatest—have written of the Trojan War. But they all go back to Homer for the basic facts and inspiration. There are no earlier records of the war.

For centuries men have argued about how much truth there is in the *Iliad*. All dates of this period are controversial, but the Trojan War is estimated to have extended from 1270 to 1260 B.C. Homer lived—if indeed he lived at all—around 775 B.C. Thus he was writing about things that happened around five hundred years before he was born.

Nothing is known of Homer himself. Tradition, probably derived from Demodocus the blind bard of the *Odyssey*, claims that Homer was blind. This is probably not true. The epics are filled with visual imagery, and the poet described details of people, life, and geography that a blind person would never have thought of. Neither Homer's birthplace nor his place of death are known either. Several places have claimed him, but none can be proved to be the real home of the greatest of the Greek poets.

Since Homer's birth is unverifiable, some claim that he is only a myth. The *Iliad* and the *Odyssey*, according to this theory, are compilations of a series of very ancient short epics handed down through the ages. Some of the best critical thought today agrees that the two epics are based upon earlier songs. But the poet known as Homer was the final compiler, and he was a poet of genius. In this theory, Homer was another Shakespeare. He took, as Shakespeare did, stories from older poets and reworked them with his own genius to produce a new work of supreme quality. If the Homeric work was not superior to those that came before it, then it would appear that they and not the *Iliad* would have survived.

In any event, the *Iliad* is not the history of the Trojan War. It tells the tragic story of a few days just before the Trojan War comes to its bitter close. Agamemnon, king of Mycenae, is jealous of Achilles, greatest of the Greeks. When Agamemnon's pride is hurt, he jealously tries to build his own ego by humbling Achilles. Achilles, in a rage, withdraws from the fighting. This almost causes the Greeks to lose the war. Now humbled himself, Agamemnon offers Achilles rich rewards to return. The wrathful hero refuses until his great friend Patroclos is killed. Then Achilles returns in all his fury and kills Hector, the heroic Trojan, in personal combat. The two armies declare a truce to bury their heroes, and the epic ends with the war still undecided.

The Greeks looked upon the *Iliad* as a bible that instructed them in all the virtues of life. In it they saw the terrible consequences of false pride. They saw the dire results of leadership that considered its own feelings before the common good. At the same time the best qualities of a man were shown in the character of Hector. Homer also showed respect for old age, respect for family life, and respect for the gods, even when they cruelly played one false.

Although its moral character is what made the *Iliad* so valuable, its popularity really depended upon its superb characterizations. The characters of the *Iliad* live, for Homer has made them human. There is no finer characterization in literature than the scene where Hector, expecting to die, says farewell to his wife and infant son. We see the tenderness between Hector and Andromaché, his wife, and his wistful hope that when his son returns from later wars men will say, "He is greater than his father."

The child is frightened by his father's helmet with its horsehair plume. He cries. We might expect a great warrior to chide the baby angrily for fear unbecoming a hero's son. But just as Homer shows the baby as a human being, so does he show the father. Hector laughs and removes the grim helmet.

And so it goes through the characters of Agamemnon, Odysseus, Achilles, Priam of Troy, and Helen, who caused it all.

The Greeks of the Classical Age looked upon the *Iliad* as true history. So did the Romans. Caesar himself thought he was a descendant of noble Trojans. But in the passing centuries, after the site of Troy was lost, scholars argued that Homer wrote fiction. They even said that there had never been a Troy at all. This view was forced to change after Heinrich Schliemann uncovered the ruins in 1870–1873. He had difficulty convincing a lot of people that he had really discovered Homer's Troy, but today all doubt has vanished. There was a Troy. Evidence of destruction and burned rocks show that there was a war at just about the time Homer said it was.

Then, as additional evidence, many of the things Homer described have been proved true. Schliemann found the site of Troy by using the geographical descriptions in the *Iliad* as his guide. This definitely proves that Homer either personally visited the site of Troy or knew someone who had. Schliemann's discovery of Nestor's Cup shows that his descriptions of the way the Mycenaeans lived had elements of truth in them. The Warrior Vase found in Mycenae depicts soldiers dressed almost exactly as Homer described them at Troy.

Carl Blegen's discovery of Nestor's palace at Pylos in 1952 added another plus for Homer. Gradually archaeology is proving the *Iliad* in parts, if not in whole. With such facts coming to light, we cannot truthfully say that there is not some historical basis for the people Homer wrote about.

The account of the Trojan War, leaving out the mythology of the gods' interference in the affairs of the two countries, gives the cause as the abduction of Helen of Sparta by Paris of Troy. Many observers have denied that a country would fight a ten-year war over a runaway queen. These observers overlook the enormous pride of these old kings and heroes. They were perfectly capable of fighting a war over a woman—or even a horse or any other possession. Only recently we have seen Ethiopia and Eritrea fighting over a piece of worthless desert as a matter of national pride.

According to the legends, when Eurystheus—who set Heracles to his labors—died, he had no heir. The Mycenaeans then chose Atreus, the son of Pelops, as the new king of Mycenae. All agree that Atreus was a good king, and honorable in all his dealing, except in his quarrels with his brother Thyestes.

After Atreus fed Thyestes' children to their father at a banquet, Thyestes cursed the house of Atreus. Curses often take a long time to come to bear, and, as it is said, the sins of the father often fall upon the children. Thus the curse of Thyestes finally fell upon the eldest son of Atreus.

After Atreus died, his son Agamemnon became king of Mycenae. His second son Menelaus was king of Sparta. The brothers married sisters. Agamemnon married Clytemnestra and Menelaus took Helen, the superlatively beautiful woman whom Theseus had kidnapped as a child.

In the course of time, Paris of Troy came to visit Menelaus. When he left, Helen went with him. The outraged king of Sparta appealed to his more powerful brother in Mycenae. Agamemnon sounded the call to arms, and the kings of the other city-states answered, altogether providing a thousand ships to punish the Trojans and bring Helen back.

At this point we come up against a difficult historical question. History tells us that Greece was never united until modern times. Each of the city-states was independent, although they often allied their fighting forces against a common enemy.

However, the fact that Agamemnon was able to call all the other Mycenaean kings to his aid has caused some scholars to claim that he was actually their overlord. This would be something like feudal England, where each baron had his own castle and army but owed allegiance to the great king in London.

This argument is not borne out by the *Iliad*. In the catalog of ships in Book II, each state is listed. There are scholars who do not believe that the catalog was written by Homer. They say that it was added later because those city-states that fought in the war wanted credit in the great epic.

Even so, the action of Achilles in refusing to fight and his withdrawing his Myrmidons from the battle shows that Agamemnon did not have the power to order this king to fight. In the end he had to give Achilles rich presents to atone for his insults.

Why then did the city-states follow Agamemnon and his brother into the war? It did not take much to make men to go to war in those days. In many places it was the custom to get out the weapons as soon as the annual crops were laid by, since the men lived as much from plunder as from husbandry.

In the case of the various Mycenaean city-states, there was racial pride. The Trojan prince had insulted them all and needed to be punished. On the other hand, Troy was a rich city. If all the Mycenaean city-states got together and sacked the place, there would be spoils aplenty for all of them. Helen, if there was a Helen, was just an excuse to men spoiling for a fight anyway.

The war between the Mycenaeans and the Trojans is said to have gone on for ten years. Homer makes it clear that the Mycenaeans never returned home during that time. But they certainly did not fight continually. They often broke off to go and attack some lesser place to get food and spoils to continue the war against Troy. This is made clear in the opening of the *Iliad*. The Mycenaeans have but recently returned from such a raid.

After their return they are stricken with a plague. Calchas, the aged soothsayer, claims this is because Agamemnon took the daughter of an old priest of Apollo as spoils of war. The priest prayed to Apollo to return his beloved child. Apollo then sent the plague, which will not go away until the girl is returned. Agamemnon gives in with ill-grace, but claims that as commander-in-chief, he should not have to give up his booty while lesser men kept theirs.

The matter could have been decided in other ways. For instance, Agamemnon could have made a sacrifice for the general good. Instead, he chose to humiliate Achilles.

In the events that follow, we get an insight into the character of the leaders on both sides. They tell stories to each other that reveal facets of Mycenaean life—accounts that archaeology partially verifies.

We learn how the Mycenaeans dressed, the utensils they used at the table, and how they acted at home. We also learn that they were not supermen. They had fears and anxieties like the rest of us. Agamemnon is so worried over the changing fortunes of war that he gets up at night to take counsel with his chiefs. Hector, great hero though he is, is afraid as he faces Achilles. Nestor, wounded and discouraged, recalls the family quarrels between his mother and father. Priam, king of Troy, is less concerned with losing his kingdom than he is with the fearful thought that the victorious Greeks will throw his dead body to the dogs to devour.

Homer has been accused of describing his own time instead of the Mycenaean age. In some cases he did make slips. He had the armies using iron swords, although the Trojan War was fought in the Middle Bronze Age. Iron was known then, but it was still a rarity and certainly not in common use in that part of the world. But Nestor's cup, inlaid swords, and many scenes painted on cups and kraters, like the Warrior Vase, show that Homer was more often right than he was wrong. We might infer from this that there was not much change—except for the introduction of iron—between the Mycenaean period and Homer's true time five hundred or so years later. Changes came slowly in those prehistoric times. Generally when they did come, it was because a conqueror imposed his own culture on a subject people.

Unfortunately, Homer's account of the Trojan War ends after the funerals of Hector of Troy and Patroclos of Greece. In the *Odyssey* there are references to the end of the war. Odysseus, having angered the gods, is forced to sail for ten years from one strange island to another before being allowed to return home. Near the end of his long odyssey he comes to the island where Alcinous is king. Odysseus does not identify himself, but his host can tell from his visitor's bearing that he is a great man.

Alcinous holds a feast for Odysseus at which a blind bard—probably the model for the accepted picture of Homer—sings a tale of Troy. Odysseus raises his cloak up before his face to hide his tears.

When Demodocus finishes singing, Odysseus says to him:

> Demodocus, I praise you above all mortal men. . . . With perfect truth you sang the lot of the Achaeans, and all they did and bore, the whole Achaean struggle, as if you yourself had been there, or you had heard the tale from one who was. Pass on now, and sing the building of the wooden horse, made by Epeis with Athena's aid, which royal Odysseus once conveyed into the Trojan citadel—a thing of craft, filled full of men, who by its means sacked Troy.

Demodocus' account of Troy's fall was only sketched in. Homer left it for later poets and storytellers to fill in the details.

The most famous account of the actual fall of the city is in Vergil's *Aeneid*. This is the story of Aeneas of the Dardanian branch of the Trojans. He escapes from Troy and goes to Italy. The *Aeneid* contains the full story of the wooden horse, which Homer only barely sketched in the *Odyssey*.

The Greeks, despairing of winning the war after Achilles is killed by an arrow shot by Paris, agree to try a trick advanced by Odysseus. They build a giant wooden horse and leave it standing on the beach as they take to their ships, as though giving up the war.

The Trojans are intrigued by the giant wooden horse. There is considerable argument about it, but they finally agree that it is an offering to the gods left behind by the Greeks. They tear down a section of the city walls to drag the horse, which is three stories high, into Troy. They do not know that Odysseus and thirty companions are hidden inside the horse.

Laocoön, a Trojan priest, tries to warn his people, saying, "I fear Greeks bearing gifts." He strikes the side of the horse with his spear to show that it is hollow.

The sea god Poseidon, who has hated Troy since Laomedon cheated him and Apollo by failing to pay for their work on the walls, sends two great serpents to strangle Laocoön and his two sons before they can convince the Trojans that the horse is a trick.

A magnificent statue showing Laocoön and his two sons struggling with the serpents is in the Vatican. It was carved in 50 B.C. by three sculptors. There is an exact replica of the statue in the royal palace on the island of Rhodes. It was made to honor the sculptors, Agesandros, Polydorus, and Athenodorus, who were born on Rhodes.

With Laocoön dead, there was no one left to warn the Trojans. They began celebrating. Then, when night fell, Odysseus and his band crept out. The Greeks came back in their ships and charged through the broken section of the wall. Attacked from within and without, the Trojan

A wooden horse, three stories high, stands at the edge of the Trojan ruins. Windows in the belly and the pagoda serve as lookout points to view the ruins.

A copy of the Lacoön group. The original is in the Vatican in Rome. This copy was made for the ducal palace on Rhodes to honor the sculptors of the original, who came from Rhodes.

resistance crumbled. The Greeks divided the plunder and sailed for home.

Historians have never agreed on what all this meant. Archaeology has forced them to admit that there was a Trojan War. The burned walls of Troy VIIa is proof of that. The fire was so hot in some places that it actually glazed the outside sections of the brick walls.

Organic material absorbs cosmic rays during its life and gives off minute bits of radioactivity after its life ends. This can be measured and compared with the radioactive decay rates to determine the age of the samples. Thus carbonized grain found in the ruins give an approximate date of the burning. This date coincides with estimates of the time of the Trojan War.

Regardless of the reason for the war, it made a deep impression upon the Greek people. They looked upon it as the most glorious exploit in their early history. Unfortunately, it was also the beginning of the end of the glory of Mycenae. Historically, no one knows what brought about the fall. But if we study the legends, it becomes clear that the fall of Mycenae came about from internal disturbances. Returning from victory at Troy, at the height of their glory, none of the Achaeans, except Odysseus, found any measure of happiness from their victory. And Odysseus had to go through ten years of trials before he could enjoy the peace of his home.

Piecing together the legends, supported by brief passages in Homer, the classical playwrights blamed much of the future Mycenaean troubles on the final working of the curse of Thyestes against the House of Atreus, which vented its fateful fury on Atreus' oldest son, Agamemnon, king of Mycenae.

7

THE FALL OF MYCENAE

Historically, Mycenae outlasted Troy by only about 150 years, but, according to legend, the destruction began the moment Troy fell. The long dormant curse of Thyestes began its cruel work, pointing directly at Agamemnon, greatest of the Mycenaean kings.

Homer in the *Odyssey* mentions only briefly what happened. When Telemachus visits Menelaus to learn what happened to his father Odysseus, the bitter king of Sparta tells him: "While I was . . . wandering, a stranger slew my brother while off guard, by stealth, and through the craft of his [Agamemnon's] cursed wife [Clytemnestra]. . . . But from your fathers you would have heard the tale, whoever they may be . . ."

This implies that the tale of Agamemnon's murder was the subject of much gossip and many stories long before Homer wrote these words. Later, when Odysseus visits Hades in the *Odyssey*, Agamemnon tells his old friend what happened: "It was Aegisthus, plotting death and doom, who slew me. He was aided by my accursed wife. . . . Saddest of all was the cry of Cassandra, Priam's daughter, whom crafty Clytemnestra slew as I on the ground lifted my hands and clutched my sword in dying."

Cassandra, the beautiful prophetess, was part of Agamemnon's booty from the sack of Troy. Her prophecies of the fall of Troy and the doom that would come to all associated with it are so vivid that her name has passed into the language. When we speak of a cassandra, it means one who predicts great misfortune and doom.

It is easy to see why the story of the Curse of Atreus should be so long remembered. It begins with murder and continues through betrayal, vengeance, more murders, matricide, and final retribution. It is all the more horrible because the entire blood drama is played out within the confines of one unhappy family group.

The background, as related earlier, is this: Pelops' sons, Atreus and Thyestes, kill a half-brother. They are banished from their father's court in Asia Minor. Both come to Argos. Then, when King Eurystheus of Mycenae dies without an heir, Atreus is elected king. His brother Thyestes becomes king of Tiryns.

This is followed by the seduction of Atreus' queen of Thyestes, and the awful revenge when Atreus feeds the flesh of Thyestes' sons to their father, who is unaware of what is happening until Atreus gloatingly reveals his terrible secret. Thyestes curses the House of Atreus.

The curse works slowly. Atreus dies and is succeeded by his son Agamemnon. Agamemnon and his brother Menelaus marry the sisters Clytemnestra and Helen. Later, while the two brothers are away fighting the war with Troy, the curse begins to work. Aegisthus, Thyestes' only surviving son, becomes the lover of Agamemnon's queen Clytemnestra. Together they plot the death of Agamemnon upon his return from Troy.

Homer says only that Aegisthus and Clytemnestra killed Agamemnon. But several Classical Age tragedians have carried on the story. These were based upon Homer and surviving legends, mixed with the writers' imagination. It is not possible at this late date to pick out the basic truth.

The classic version of the tragedy of the House of Atreus is the *Oresteia*—the story of Orestes, son of Agamemnon, written by Aeschylus. Aeschylus was a member of a prominent Athenian family. He fought at Marathon in 490 B.C. to help halt the Persian invasion under Darius the Great. Ten years later, in 480 B.C., he was in the battle of Salamis, which stemmed another Persian invasion, this time under Xerxes, son of Darius. He was sixty-six years old in 458 B.C. when he wrote the *Oresteia*. He changed the setting from Mycenae to nearby Argos. There may have been a political motive in this change. Athens was then allied with Argos against Sparta.

The first of the three plays in the trilogy that make up the *Oresteia* is *Agamemnon*. The play opens on the roof of the palace, where a watchman looks toward the mountains in the direction of faraway Troy. He is complaining because Clytemnestra, the queen, posts him here every night to watch for a sign from Troy. Suddenly he sees a torchlight flare on the mountaintop beyond the city. He cries out in joy, calling to Clytemnestra. He observes that this is a sign that Agamemnon has triumphed in Troy. He also hints that something is amiss. He will not talk himself, "but if the palace itself could talk, it could tell quite a tale."

Clytemnestra, getting word of the torchlight from the watchman, informs the city council that Troy has fallen that night. They ask how she knows. The queen tells them that arrangements were made to light a torch atop Mount Ida near Troy as soon as victory was achieved. There was another sentinel on Mount Hermes on the island of Lemnos. And so it went. Fires were lighted on mountaintop after mountaintop, all within sight of each other, until the watcher on the roof saw the fire blaze up on Mount Arachnaeon on the edge of the Plain of Argos.

Soon Agamemnon arrives with his twenty-man guard, the first of the Mycenaeans to return from Troy. He enters in a chariot, followed by a wagon carrying his loot from the war. Among this is Cassandra, the prophetess daughter of Priam of Troy. The Greek chorus bids him welcome. Then Clytemnestra adds her welcome and tries to get Agamemnon to walk into the palace on an embroidered red carpet she has rolled out for him. He objects that it is unseemly to do so. In the exchange between them it is clear that each hates the other.

Agamemnon marches into the palace, after leaving word that Cassandra is to be treated well. After some contemptuous words to Cassandra, Clytemnestra follows Agamemnon into the palace.

Cassandra descends from her wagon and embraces a statue of Apollo, to whom she is a priestess. She begins hysterically to recall the beginning of the Curse on Atreus, when Atreus fed Thyestes the cooked flesh of his own children. Then she prophesizes another murder, committed by a woman against a man in his bath. Several times she repeats this prophecy, but the Greek chorus—representing the council—cannot understand what she means, although they understand the references to Atreus and Thyestes.

Cassandra then prophesizes her own death. She strips away her priestess's gown and walks into the palace. Shortly there is a cry from inside the palace. Agamemnon is shouting that he has been struck a fatal blow. As the chorus—the councillors—are debating what to do, Clytemnestra is revealed by the opening of the palace doors. She is standing by a silver bathtub in which the dead body of Agamemnon is sprawled. Cassandra lies dead on the floor.

She defiantly—even proudly—tells the councillors that she struck two blows to kill her husband. And then struck a third blow, because three is a lucky number. She turns back their reproaches. She justifies her actions as part of the curse of Thyestes, and accuses Agamemnon of sacrificing their daughter Iphigenia, which he did, to gain a strong wind to blow their ships to Troy.

At this point Aegisthus enters and proclaims that this is a day of judgment. Agamemnon has paid in full for his father's (Atreus') crime against Thyestes, Atreus' brother.

The chorus accuses Aegisthus of lacking the courage to kill Agamemnon himself. He replies that Agamemnon knew him for an enemy. It was necessary for Clytemnestra to do the deed. Then he declares he will now rule in Agamemnon's place, and all who oppose him will feel his yoke.

Aegisthus' bodyguard and Agamemnon's soldiers face each other. It appears that there will be a fight, but Clytemnestra orders them to disperse. They follow her orders. She tells Aegisthus that they will rule Argos together.

The play ends at this point, but the tragedy has yet to run its bloody course. The next stage comes in the second play of the trilogy, *The Libation Bearers*.

Clytemnestra and Agamemnon had a young son, Orestes, and a daughter, Electra. Orestes was away when his father was killed and never returned. The boy was thirteen years old. Under the blood code of the Mycenaeans, he was duty bound to avenge the murder of his father.

Yet, to do so, he must murder his mother. This is a horrible crime. This places the boy in an impossible position.

As *The Libation Bearers* opens, Orestes, now twenty years old, secretly returns in the company of his friend Pylades. He goes to the grave of his father and cuts a lock of his hair. This is placed upon the grave. It is a traditional way to show respect for a corpse. In the *Iliad* all the Achaeans pass by the body of Patroclus and drop a lock of their hair onto the corpse.

A Greek chorus, led by Orestes' sister Electra, comes to pour libations of wine on the grave of Agamemnon. The two men hide and then Orestes reveals himself to Electra. The chorus warns him that he is endangered by returning. He replies that Apollo has told him of all the troubles that come to one who fails to avenge a relative's death. Therefore, by Apollo's command and his own love of his father, plus his hunger to take his rightful place on the Mycenaean throne, he must carry out his pledge of blood vengeance.

The chorus agrees that bloodshed demands more bloodshed. Orestes' revenge focuses upon Aegisthus, but Electra, bitterly hating her mother Clytemnestra, tells Orestes how Clytemnestra denied Agamemnon his rightful funeral honors. He was buried like an enemy, without procession and songs.

Orestes now plans his revenge. He goes to the palace. Clytemnestra does not recognize him. He tells her that a man he met in his travels asked that he stop in Mycenae to inform Orestes' family that the boy is dead.

While Clytemnestra weeps for her dead son, the chorus informs Aegisthus. He is suspicious and wishes to question the stranger who brought the news. He goes with his serving boy to see Orestes. This is followed by Aegisthus' offstage screams as he is killed by the vengeful youth. The servant runs to tell Clytemnestra that the dead are killing the living. She calls for a weapon so that she can avenge her lover's death.

Orestes, carrying the bloodstained sword that killed Aegisthus, confronts his mother. She weeps for Aegisthus. Orestes cries that if she still loves Aegisthus, then they can lie in the same grave. She pleads for her life, but her vengeful son replies that in killing her husband she did what she should not have done. Therefore he has no choice but to do what he should not do. He forces her into the guest room, where the murder occurs offstage.

He returns with servants carrying the dead bodies of the guilty pair. They lie side by side. Orestes tries to justify the murder of his mother by claiming that Apollo urged him to do it. While the chorus moans, Orestes sees the Furies, the hideous women-monsters who pursue the guilty. The others cannot see them and claim that it is all his fancy. He knows better, and the chorus urges him to seek purification in Apollo's temple. He runs out as the chorus pitifully asks where all this will end.

The Libation Bearers ends at this point. Like a serial, it leaves the audience in an agony of suspense as to the fate of the hero.

Others who have retold the story have all followed the basic outline, so we can presume that this much is true: Agamemnon was killed by Clytemnestra and Aegisthus. Orestes did return to take revenge. The details were altered to fit each poet's purpose. In *Electra*, Euripides (480–413 B.C.) tells the story a little differently. He chooses Electra as his central character. After Agamemnon's death, Aegisthus fears that if she is married in her own class, she will produce a son who may seek revenge. So he has her married to an aged peasant.

Orestes returns, seeking revenge. He meets Electra at a spring and reveals himself. They plot revenge. Orestes goes to a meadow where Aegisthus is performing a sacrifice. The king invites the stranger to join him in the ceremony. The omens from the sacrifice indicate doom. Startled, Aegisthus peers more closely at the sacrificial animal as Orestes kills him with a sword.

Orestes reveals himself and is hailed by the servants. The body is taken to Electra's hut. In the meantime Electra has sent word to her mother that she has given birth. Clytemnestra rushes to the hut in a chariot. Orestes is hidden within to kill his mother as she enters. His courage fails, but when Electra scorns him for it, he agrees to go ahead.

Clytemnestra enters the hut. Electra follows, intending to strike a blow herself. She falters when Clytemnestra cries for mercy, but Orestes stabs his mother in the throat.

A vision appears in the sky. It declares that Clytemnestra's death was righteous, but the murder itself by her children was not. Electra is taken from her aged husband and married to Orestes' friend Pylades. The two are sent into exile as her punishment. (Exile was considered a very harsh punishment in those days.) Orestes is told to go to Athens and pray to Apollo to remove his terrible sin.

Aeschylus carries on his story in *The Furies*, which tells of how Orestes suffers and then finds peace. The final play in the trilogy opens at Apollo's Oracle of Delphi. The priestess finishes her oracles for the people at the entrance. She turns and enters the building. Then she rushes back out, screaming in terror. In front of Apollo's golden statue she sees a man holding a bloodstained sword. He is surrounded by foul, monstrous women who are screaming accusations at him. It is Orestes pursued by the Furies.

Apollo comes and puts the Furies to sleep. Then he tells Orestes that he will watch over the unfortunate man. The god admits that it was he who urged Orestes to murder his mother. He orders Orestes to go to Athens, where he will find judges to hear his case.

After Apollo and Orestes depart, the vengeful ghost of Clytemnestra arouses the Furies from their sleep. The Furies blame Apollo for Orestes' action and denounce the god for interfering with their duty to hound one who has murdered his mother. Apollo returns and orders them from his temple. They are furious at his interference. Apollo asks why they pursue Orestes, but did not do the same to Clytemnestra and Aegisthus. They reply that neither Clytemnestra nor Aegisthus killed one of kindred blood. The god claims this is a poor defense for their actions. They retort that it is not up to him to question their actions. It is their duty to hound Orestes for killing his mother.

Orestes, pursued by the hounding Furies, goes to Athens and embraces the statue of Athena. She appears. The Furies insist that they have come from the Underworld to do their duty. They and Orestes expect her to decide the fate of Orestes, but she says it would not be right for her to do so. Instead she will appoint men from her people and have them sit on Aeropagus, the hill between the Acropolis and the Agora in Athens.

(This is the legend of the founding of the first Supreme Court in Greece.)

At the trial of Orestes, the argument is that it is the father who supplies the blood of a child. The mother is only the receptacle and the nurse for the baby. The voting of the judges is a tie, and under the rules this constitutes acquittal. Orestes is free from the persecution of the *Furies*.

Although Aeschylus laid his story in Argos, tradition says that Orestes came back to Mycenae and took the throne of the murdered Agamemnon. Pausanias reported that Agamemnon was buried inside the walls, but that Clytemnestra and Aegisthus were not considered worthy of such an honor and were buried outside the walls. It was this passage from Pausanias that led Schliemann to find the golden graves in Grave Circle A, just inside the Lion Gate of Mycenae.

Two beehive-shaped tombs outside the walls are still called the tombs of Clytemnestra and Aegisthus. Unfortunately, archaeology does not agree with tradition. A study of the architecture shows that the tombs were built 250 years apart.

These beehive tombs—called *tholos* tombs—are highly impressive examples of Mycenaean architecture. They were constructed by digging into the side of a hill. Then stones were laid in courses (circles), each layer toeing in like an Eskimo igloo to come to a point at the top. A stone-lined approach to the entrance followed the curve of the hill. The entrance itself was highly decorated.

The most famous of these tombs is the so-called Treasury of Atreus. It is dug into a hill that looks across a valley to the ruins of the citadel of Mycenae. The tomb received its name from the local tradition that the father of Agamemnon was buried there.

The entrance and interior today are only bare stone. But originally they were both highly decorated. The entrance itself was of stone blocks topped by a huge stone lintel. Above the lintel was the same kind of relieving triangle to reduce pressure that we saw in the Lion Gate. However, this one is not carved, for the entire face of the entrance was decorated with inlaid marble of different colors. Two half columns of green stone were set on each side. The doors were of wood, studded with bronze.

Mycenae as seen from the Treasury of Atreus.

Inside, holes in the stones show that the walls were decorated with rosettes of bronze. This may have been the origin of the "bronze walls" referred to by early writers.

The tomb tradition assigns to Aegisthus was very primitive and crudely made. That assigned to Clytemnestra was built in the same period as the so-called Treasury of Atreus, estimated to be between 1400 and 1350 B.C. This tomb appears to have been built from eighty to a hundred years before the Trojan War and the time of the real Clytemnestra, but it does appear to have been a queen's tomb. The site was originally excavated by Sophia Schliemann, who found a golden mirror and some other articles which indicated that it had been a woman's tomb.

The shaft graves where Schliemann found the golden masks and other treasures were much older than the beehive tombs. However, it appears that the burial ceremonies were very much the same. The body was carried to the grave site by members of the family. The body was fully clothed, but was not placed in a coffin in this period. Food and personal treasures were arranged around the body. Sacrifices were made and libations poured.

A painting on stone found in Crete shows a sacrificial ceremony for the dead as it was practiced during the Mycenaean period of the island. In one of the scenes, three men, wearing animal-skin skirts, are carrying presents to the dead man. Behind them two women are bringing buckets of sacrificial blood to a priestess who is pouring blood into a sacred vessel on an altar. Another scene shows a priestess sacrificing a bull tied to an altar, while a vase on the floor catches the blood pouring from its neck wound. A man plays a flute behind the sacrificial animal, while another priestess seems to be calling the gods at an altar.

This lion's head rhyton used for blood libations was found in Grave Circle A at Mycenae.

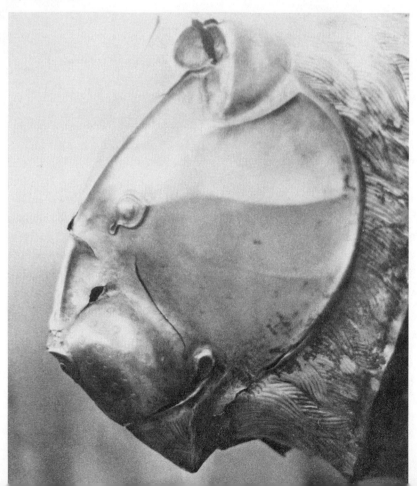

The so-called Tomb of Aegisthus is an early example of the tholos *tomb and is not as impressive as the tombs of Clytemnestra and Atreus.*

After the burial, the tomb was closed. However, it appears that the tombs were for family, rather than individual, use. When another member of the family died, the tomb was reopened. In the case of the small pit graves and chamber tombs, this was not much of a problem, but the dead air caused by the putrefaction of the bodies in the large beehive tombs was unendurable. The tombs had to be purified by huge bonfires lighted inside the tombs before the ceremony for the new body could be held.

Two examples of the pit graves opened by Schliemann in Grave Circle A at Mycenae.

The old body or bodies were moved to one side and the new corpse was always placed in the center.

In Grave Circle A, where Schliemann found the golden masks, the burial customs go back about three hundred years earlier than the beehive tombs, being dated around 1600 B.C., the time when the Mycenaeans were first making their mark in the world.

However, the burial customs were much the same as in the later period. The pits were dug in the ground and lined with rock or were chiseled from solid rock. Then a three-foot wall was constructed inside. This was to hold timber covers to keep the dirt from falling on the bodies when the grave was filled. The floor of the grave was covered with pebbles. The fully clothed body was lowered into the grave. If this was a later burial, the other bodies were moved to one side to make room. Personal treasures were placed beside the corpse, the wooden cover placed to protect them, and the grave filled. Then a banquet was held and the pottery cups used in the toasts to the dead were shattered on the grave mound.

The Mycenaeans believed that the soul of the dead went to the Underworld presided over by Hades. However, the soul remained on earth until its body decomposed, during which period it could cause harm to the living. This is why the dead person's treasures were placed beside it. The spirit would be pleased and less inclined to take its spite out on the living. However, once the spirit had gone to the House of Hades, the Greek Hell, it could never return and was no longer a threat to the living.

Hades was not a place of punishment, but it was apparently not a happy place. When Odysseus visited there, the spirit of Achilles told him bitterly that it was better to be a slave in the living world than a king in Hades.

8

HOW THE MYCENAEANS LIVED

If a dead Mycenaean was an important person, then the burial was often followed by games at which the family or friends of the deceased gave rich prizes to the winners.

These funeral games followed the same plan and rules of the contests Homer's Greeks held both for fun and for military training. They were the forerunners of the Olympic Games, which were first held in 776 B.C. The best description of funeral games is in the *Iliad*. Here Homer not only tells us how the games were played, but shows us the temper and craftiness of those who competed. We see their sportsmanship as well.

Although Homer has time and again been proved right in what he said about the Mycenaeans, there is a big difference in his description of a funeral and what we have learned from the excavations of the tholos, chamber, and pit tombs. These prove definitely that the Mycenaeans buried their dead. Homer has the bodies of Patroclus and Hector cremated. Furthermore, he says definitely that fire is their due.

It has been suggested that Homer was describing the funeral customs of his own time—five hundred or so years later. This is doubtful. Homer was certainly aware of the great tombs around Greece and that general cremation was not the custom even in his own time. We can suspect that Patroclus and Hector were burned as part of military rites, since in a foreign country graves might not be properly honored.

The first event in the games honoring Patroclus at Troy was a chariot race. As the entrants make ready, Homer lets us listen in on King Nestor giving advice to his son:

Antilochus, you know well how to wheel around the post. Yet your horses are slow for a race. Therefore, I think this will be sad work for you. Yet, although their horses are faster, the men are not as cunning as you. . . . By cunning does a helmsman on the wine-dark sea steer his swift ship buffeted by winds. By cunning is one charioteer better than another.

Nestor went on to advise his son how to take the inside track, bringing his wheel close to the turn marker. But, he cautioned, not so close that he would smash his wheel. The young man listened carefully and then went to the lineup, where five chariots were entered. The drivers drew lots for the starting positions. Then they waited with whips upraised for Achilles to signal the start.

They rolled out with a shout. Dust boiled up from their wheels. Homer tells us that the chariots bounced in the air as they hit rough ground. The poet says:

The drivers stood up in the cars. The heart of every man beat in the desire of victory. Every man called to his horses, that flew amid the dust across the plain. But when the fleet horses were running the last part of the course, back toward the gray sea, then was manifest the prowess of each.

The number-two chariot was so close to the front runner that the charioteer could feel the breath of the oncoming horses on his back. Then the front runner lost his whip and his horses faltered. Homer blames this accident upon the interference of the god Apollo. Then the chariot tongue broke on the leading chariot.

The mares ran sidewise off the course, and the pole was twisted to the ground. And Eumelos [the driver] was hurled out of the car beside the wheel. His elbows and mouth and nose were flayed, and his forehead bruised above the eyebrows. His eyes filled with tears and his lusty voice was choked.

Now Tydeides took the lead for the goddess Athene put spirit into his steeds and shed glory on himself. Now next after him came golden-haired Menelaus, Atreus' son. But Antilochus called to his father's horses.

A grave marker shows the beginning of a chariot race like the one described by Homer. The groom at the left helps restrain the horses until the start signal.

Antilochus knew that he could not overtake the leader, but he began shouting to his own horses. He wanted second place. He reminded his team that Menelaus was driving a mare in his team. She would heap scorn on the stallions if she beat them. Then he promised that Nestor would slay them with his sword if they failed to put out their best.

On the straightaway they headed into a bad section where a stream had eaten across the course. Menelaus cautiously slowed his chariot to avoid an upset. But Antilochus rushed in at full speed. It was a narrow section and the two chariots came so close to crashing together that Menelaus, shouting angrily at Antilochus, pulled back to avoid disaster to both chariots.

The dust from the chariot wheels was so thick the spectators could not see well. Two of them got into a quarrel over which chariot was ahead and quickly made a bet between themselves.

The winning chariot, driven by Sthenelos, rolled in, followed by Antilochus in second place and a fuming Menelaus coming in third.

Menelaus immediately challenged Antilochus' right to second prize. He demanded that the prize—a fine mare—be given to him. He admitted that the spectators had not seen the reckless way Antilochus cut off Menelaus' chariot and they would think "through false words has Menelaus gone off with the mare." He challenged Antilochus to place his whip on his chariot and swear that he had not interfered.

This Antilochus refused to do. He pleaded the rashness of youth, apologized to Menelaus, and gave him the mare. Menelaus, overcome by the youth's apology, returned the mare to Antilochus. Thus a quarrel that might have had serious consequences was averted.

To make doubly sure that Nestor, Antilochus' father, who had advised his son to be crafty, did not take offense, Achilles gave the last prize, for which there was no claimant, to Nestor. He personally carried the two-handled cup to the king, saying it was awarded in honor of his age.

Nestor, pleased, recalled his youth when he won prizes at the funeral games of another hero:

> Then was no man found like me [he boasted]. In boxing I overcame Kyltomedes, and in wrestling Ankaios, and in the footrace I outran Ipiklos, a right good man, and with the spear outthrew Plyleus and Polydoros. . . . Thus was I once, but now let younger men join in such feats. I must bend to grievous age.

Homer's Greeks were mainly nobility or aristocrats. Servants and slaves move in and out of the picture, but the poet has little to say about the common man. Nor does he say anything about commerce or business. We know that the original Mycenaeans were herdsmen and farmers. Some remained so. The *Odyssey* tells of the vast flocks and herds owned by Odysseus. However, after 1600 B.C. a working class of artisans grew up. Mycenaean pottery was exported as far away as Eygpt.

Iron forgers and smelters were developed. Copper, tin, iron, and gold were imported and worked. The large number of ships used in the Trojan War and in the wide commerce on the sea indicates that shipbuilding must have been a very important industry. Wrecks of ships found by skin divers show that there was a wide traffic in imports of grain, oils, and wine. The need for containers for these caused the pottery business to boom.

The only descriptions Homer gave of everyday work were limited to house servants, shepherds, and soldiers. When he talked of artisans, he usually described the work as performed by gods or nobility.

For example, needlework was highly prized. In some cases where women slaves were given as prizes, mention was made of their sewing accomplishments. Just as Odysseus, a king, and Paris, a prince, herded part of their flocks, the queens and princesses sewed and embroidered. When Helen is called to the Scaean gates to identify the Greeks for Priam, we are told: "And in the hall she found Helen weaving a great purple web of double fold, and embroidering thereon many battles of horse-taming Trojans and mail-clad Achaeans."

Homer provides us a very good description of an armorer at work. The workman is Hephaestus, armorer of the gods, and he speaks of making bronze work, brooches, spiral arm bands, cups, and necklaces. From this we can assume that the Vaphio cups, Nestor's Cup, the priestess ring, the golden masks, and other treasures found by excavators were made locally and were not Cretan imports.

Homer first described Hephaestus putting away his tools:

> The bellows he set away from the fire, and gathered all his gear wherewith he worked and put it in a silver chest. And with a sponge he wiped his face and hands and sturdy neck and shaggy breast.

Later Homer describes a great shield that Hephaestus makes for Achilles. This is a very important passage in the *Iliad*, for the armorer decorates the shield with embossed scenes and figures that are almost a complete picture of life in Homer's time. It is one of the few times that the great poet gives much indication of how others than the aristocracy lived. But first he described the forging of the shield.

There were twenty bellows—probably pumped by slaves—to supply blasts of air to the forging fire.

> Then he threw bronze that weareth not into the fire, and tin and precious gold and silver. Next he set a great anvil on an anvil-stand, and took in his hand a sturdy hammer, and in the other he took the tongs. . . . First he fashioned a shield, great and strong. . . . Five were the folds of the shield itself.

One of the ways that metal was forged and hardened was to heat it until it was red-hot and reasonably soft. This was hammered down and then folded over and the fold welded together by hammering the red-hot metal. Homer indicates that the shield was made of five layers of red-hot metal hammer-forged together to make an exceptionally strong shield.

Then the armorer began adding the decorations. Among these were

> two fair cities of mortal men. In the one were espousals and marriage feasts. Beneath the lighted torches they were leading the brides from their chambers through the city. Loud arose the bridal song. And young men were whirling in the dance. And among them flutes and viols sounded high. Women standing each at her door were marvelling.

In another place two men were arguing over the blood price to be paid for a man who had been killed. When the two were unable to agree, the problem was passed to a council of elders to decide.

Then the second city depicted was shown with armies in siege. Scouts from the army lay in ambush to catch returning herdsmen:

> And presently came the cattle, and with them two herdsmen playing on pipes, that took no thought of guile. Then the soldiers when they beheld these ran upon them and quickly cut off the herd of oxen and fair flocks of white sheep, and killed the shepherds withal.

From this we get a picture of how the Achaeans got their provisions for their long siege of Troy. After showing some battle scenes, the pictures turned bucolic—farmers plowing a field:

> . . . a soft fresh-ploughed field, rich and wide, the third time ploughed. Many ploughers therein drove their yokes of oxen to and fro as they wheeled about. When they came to the boundary of the field and turned, then would a man come to each of them and give unto his hands a goblet of sweet wine. Others would be turning back along the furrows, eager to reach the boundary.
>
> Furthermore there was a demesne-land of a king, where reapers were cutting with sharp sickles in their hands. Armfuls along the swathe were falling in rows to the earth. These the sheaf-binders were binding in twisted bands of straw. . . . Among them the king in silence was standing at the swathe with his staff, rejoicing in his heart. Henchmen apart beneath an oak tree were making ready a feast, preparing a great ox they had sacrificed. Women were stewing much white barley to be a supper for the reapers.
>
> Also Hephaistus set therein a vineyard teeming plenteously with cluster, wrought fair in gold. Black were the grapes, but the vines hung from silver poles. . . . Maidens and striplings in childish glee carried the fruit in plaited baskets. And in the midst of them a boy made pleasant music on a clear-toned viol, and sang thereto a sweet Linos-song. The rest, with feet falling together, kept time with the music and song.

Homer does not mention it himself, but from Hesiod, a poet of the time of Homer, we learn how the strong Greek wine was made. This wine was rarely drunk straight, but was diluted with water. Those who did not water their wine were looked upon as alcoholics.

The grapes were dried for six days in the sun. They were then placed in big vats and crushed by trampling bare feet. The vat was placed in the shade to ferment for exactly five days. This made a thick concentrate, high in sugar and alcohol content. The thickness was caused by drying the water for days before the grapes were crushed. This thickness and strength required the liquor to be diluted with water before it was served.

In his description of the shield Hephaestus made for Achilles Homer includes a picture of the dangers of herding cattle. Four herdsmen and nine dogs came upon two lions who had:

seized a loud-roaring bull that bellowed mightily as they attacked him.
The dogs and the young men sped to them. The lions were rending the
great bull's hide and devouring his vitals, and his black blood. The
herdsmen in vain urged their dogs on. The dogs shrank back from
attacking the lions, but stood hard by and barked and swerved away.

Less violent aspects of pastoral life in Homer's time were shown:

> Hephaistus also wrought there a pasture in a fair glen, a great pasture of
> white sheep, and a steading, and roofed huts, and folds.
> Also did the glorious lame god devise a dancing-place like unto that
> which once in wide Knossus Daedalus wrought for Ariadne of the lovely
> tresses.

This would indicate that Mycenaean artisans and craftsmen locally
copied Cretan Minoan designs, giving support for the theory that the
Vaphio cups and other Minoan designs and paintings found in Mycenae
and Tiryns were the work of Greek artists and not of masters imported
from Knossus. It also gives some literary evidence of the close ties
between the Minoans and the early Mycenaeans, bolstering the argument that the Minoans from Knossus were the teachers who lifted the
Mycenaeans from simple herdsmen to a feudal civilization.

Homer continues:

> There were youths dancing and maidens of costly wooing, their hands
> upon one another's wrists. Fine linen the maidens had on, and the youths
> well-woven doublets faintly glistening with oil. Fair wreaths had the
> maidens, and the youths daggers of gold hanging from silver baldrics.
> And now would they run around with deft feet exceedingly light, as when
> a potter sitting by his wheel makes a trial of it. And now anon they would
> run in lines to meet each other. A great company stood around the lovely
> dance in joy. Among them a divine minstrel was making music on his
> lyre. Through the midst of them, leading the measure, two tumblers
> whirled.

The references to the gold daggers and silver baldrics are to the work
on the shield. Actually, Homer was describing a country folk dance of a
type that can still be seen in Greece today.

In his description of Achilles' shield Homer mentions all classes and activities of the people of his time. If this seems an impossible number of figures to engrave, emboss, or chase onto a single shield, we have only to look at the delicacy of the work on some of the gold rings found in the Mycenaean treasure to see how minutely these wonderful gold- and silversmiths could work. The famous priestess finger ring included five figures, a tree, a floating god, emblems of the sun, moon, and seas, six odd shapes that have not been identified, and a double ax. All this was modeled in a space of a little over an inch in length.

The intriguing thing about Homer's description of Achilles' shield is that the poet has been proved right in some of his other descriptions. This one is so detailed and carries such a ring of truth that we can well believe that he is describing something he really saw—as he did with Nestor's Cup. It could well be that this treasure of treasures still lies buried in some forgotten part of the Mycenaean world. As a treasure, it would be greater than any of the others found in Greece, because it would show us, as an artist of the time saw it, the everyday life of the real Greeks of the Homeric age.

The picture of the shepherd's home (" . . .in a fair glen . . . a steading, and roofed huts . . .") is a pretty close description of the grazing houses one sees in driving between Athens and Delphi today. These houses are built of rocks picked up from the hills and mortared with clay or cement. They generally have thatched roofs and are surrounded by rock walls to act as an enclosure for the sheep or goats being herded. They are used during the spring grazing season, and then, when the lack of summer rain destroys the grazing, the flocks are driven to other pastures. These houses are perched in hollows high on the hills and have no access roads, approachable only by sheep and goat paths.

We know much more about the Mycenaean palaces than about the homes of the common people. Homer has left a number of descriptions of the palaces of Odysseus on Ithaca, Nestor at Pylos, Menelaus at Sparta, and Agamemnon at Mycenae. We can add to these descriptions the information gathered by archaeological excavations.

The palace at Mycenae, judging by its ruins, was the most imposing of them all. The Lion Gate and the great wall were near the foot of the hill.

A great stone ramp led from the base of the Lion Gate to the acropolis on top of the hill. The acropolis, where the temples and the palace were located, was surrounded by still another wall. Houses of the lesser nobility and high officials were jammed on the hill between the acropolis walls and the lower Lion Gate walls.

The palace at Mycenae was destroyed—tradition places it as eighty years after the return from Troy. Later temples were constructed on the spot, which destroyed some of the foundations of the palace. However, considerable excavation work has been done on the summit, and the general outlines of Agamemnon's home have come to light.

The grand palaces of these times were really small cities in themselves. They included not only the living quarters of the king and his family, but quarters for his servants, storage rooms, stables, livestock

The palace of the Mycenaean kings was behind this wall at the top of the fortified hill. Ruins of a house built by the lesser nobility cover the ground below the wall.

pens, and quarters for his guards. According to Homer, Priam's palace at Troy had fifty rooms for his sons and their wives, and an extra twelve for his married daughters and his sons-in-law. These were in addition to the king's own quarters for himself, his queen (who had her own room), and his concubines. There were also halls, public council rooms, and offices.

In addition to the acropolis wall, there was an additional wall around the palace itself. A visitor entered through the grand entrance, or *propylon*, which was in front of the real entrance. This was approached between two guardhouses set on a terrace below the wall.

There was a courtyard inside the palace, but the building was actually built around the *megaron*. This was the great formal hall. The other rooms led off from it with grand stairways to the upper stories.

Women's quarters were arranged on three sides of the megaron. These included, although separated from each other, rooms for both the servant women and the king's family. The women also worked in these rooms, spinning, weaving, cooking, and taking care of other everyday chores.

The king's sleeping quarters, separated from the queen's, was inside the women's quarters. This appears to have been a safety precaution. Any assassin trying to attack the king would have to weave his way through the various women's rooms before he could approach the king's bedroom. "Uneasy lies the head that wears a crown," as Shakespeare put it, applied to kings from the very beginning of royalty.

Most of the walls were covered with paintings. Some were frescoes— that is, painted into wet plaster—and some were dry painted. Because of the great fire and destruction when Mycenae fell, the paintings found were not as extensive or as well preserved as those of Tiryns. Two of the Tiryns paintings are exceptional. One is a fragment of a boar hunt. The other shows two young women driving a chariot.

The megaron, or great ceremonial hall, dominated the palace. It served not only as a gathering place for formal events, but also as the throne room and the dining hall. Small tables were brought in and grouped together for the meals and banquets, and then removed.

The megaron at Mycenae had a small porch that opened onto a courtyard. Visitors passed through a door flanked by two columns into a

A fresco painting found in Tiryns shows two young women driving a chariot. The painting is now in the National Archaeological Museum in Athens.

small room that served as a vestibule. There were benches in the room and a staircase leading to the rooms above. The *domos*, or central hall, was almost square in shape. The walls were painted and the floor paved with stone.

In the center of the megaron was an open hearth about nine feet in diameter. The hearth was built up of stones several inches from the floor and the sides of the stones were painted with a design of flames and spirals. Four columns were set around the hearth and these supported the roof. There was a hole in the roof for the smoke to rise through. A raised hood above this hole kept out rain.

The columns have not survived, but archaeologists have found the stone bases upon which they rested. The columns, like those of Knossus, were made of wood. They would have been destroyed in the great fire that destroyed the palace.

We know from the *Odyssey* that there were arms racks around the megaron walls, for Odysseus and his son removed the weapons before they attacked the suitors who were trying to marry Penelope, Odysseus' wife.

The Greeks of all ages and times have been fond of travel. The lords of the manor were delighted to entertain visiting guests, from whom they gathered news of other cities and far-off places. A visitor could always depend upon being given a banquet by his peers.

These were held in the megaron. There were only a few chairs—called thrones—and they were reserved for the more distinguished guests. The others sat on benches or low divans; however, they did not recline as they ate, like the later Romans.

Meat and wheat bread were the heart of the banquet meals. The better pieces were roasted over spit fires. The less tender pieces were boiled in caldrons hung over metal tripods. Bread was griddle-baked on iron sheets. Before the introduction of iron, bread was often cooked on hot, flat stones. Later it was baked in ovens.

Although meat was the staple of the Mycenaean diet, they also ate honey, fruits, and vegetables. Homer's Greeks were very fond of dried figs, which could be kept and eaten long after the fruit season had ended. They also ate a lot of cheese, mostly goat cheese, but they do not seem to have drunk milk. This is probably because it turned bad so quickly without refrigeration. Cheese was the alternate.

In the *Odyssey*, the chapter on the Cyclopes, Homer gives a description of cheese making. In much the same manner of American farmers fifty years ago, the lambs and kids were kept away from the milk ewes and nannies. The flocks were driven in at night and milked. Then the kids were released to ''strip'' the remaining milk from the udders.

The milk for cheese was placed in pottery jugs to curdle. The curds were then transferred to woven baskets, which permitted the whey (water) to drip out. The resulting milk solids were kneaded and pressed to force out the remaining water. The resulting mass was placed on trays to ferment and dry.

For some reason, Homer's Greeks did not eat fish. Possibly this was because Mycenae was too far from the coast to keep the fish fresh in transport. But this theory does not explain why the people of seaside Tiryns also did not eat fish.

Along the coast there were fishing villages where inhabitants lived on seafood. However, these people seemed to have been looked upon as inferior by those who lived in the great castle towns.

These city-states did not have long lives. They were always quarreling with their neighbors and fighting among themselves. Mycenae's period of importance lasted about five hundred years—from 1600 B.C. to 1100 B.C. Then the citadel was destroyed, although life continued, apparently, in the lower part of the town.

The end was sudden and mysterious. There have been many theories, but no one really knows what caused the downfall of this greatest of the Mycenaean cities.

9

THE DARK YEARS

The destruction of Mycenae was shockingly swift and mysterious. Some investigators have tried to explain the fall in terms of the *Oresteia*, the story of Orestes' revenge for the murder of Agamemnon. This, they say, created internal dissensions and civil strife that weakened the city-state, making it an easy prey to its neighbors.

In seeking to find clues in traditions and legends, we have little help here. The traditions are conflicting. Some say that Orestes never returned to Mycenae. But others say he did take the throne of his murdered father. He lived out his years and was succeeded by his son. According to archaeologist S. E. Jakovidis, "The last king of Mycenae, according to tradition, was Tisamenos, Orestes' son. He was killed while defending his country from an incursion by the Heraclids." The Heraclids were the descendents of Heracles, once king of nearby Tiryns.

Somewhere around 1200 B.C. there were great fires and signs of destruction in Mycenae. Although all dates in ancient history are highly controversial, this would appear to be about fifty to eighty years after the supposed date of the Trojan War and would agree timewise with the legend that Orestes' son was king of Mycenae at the fall. However, other archaeological evidence shows that this damage, great as it was, did not destroy the city. The destruction was repaired. Excavations have shown that the city did not regain its former power and greatness. From this time until about 1100 B.C., there was a gradual decline. After 1100 B.C. Mycenae ceased to be of importance in the affairs of the Plain of Argos.

Mycenae, of course, was only one city-state in the region. It gave its name to the entire area—which is called Mycenaean—because of its original power.

However, the destruction by fire that hit Mycenae about 1200 B.C. was apparently widespread. According to Konstantinos Kontorlis (in *Mycenaean Civilization*),

> Around 1200 B.C. . . . whole or partial destructions by fire are found in the settlements of mainland Greece: at Krisa in Phicos, at Gla in Boeotia, at Zygouries in Corinthia, at Mycenae and Tiryns in the Argolid, at Pylus in Messenia, and at the Menelaion in Laconia.

He also points out that a number of Mycenaean settlements were destroyed at this time and never rebuilt. During the same period, archaeological evidence shows that there was an increase in population in Attica (the area around Athens), in Achaea (the province of the Peloponnesus bordering on the Gulf of Corinth), and on the island of Cyprus.

We cannot draw from this an inference of an invader, although for years historians held the belief that the destruction was due to the invading Dorians, barbaric Greeks from the north. Nor can we say that it was due to civil war between Mycenae and those sections of Greece that showed a population increase. The increase was probably due to refugees from the great Mycenaean centers.

As to an invader, Kontorlis says,

> The archaeological record does not show anything like the arrival of new peoples. It reveals no new weapons around the destroyed sites and no new elements of a foreign culture. The survivors in all districts, and especially in the Argolid, Messenia and Laconia, maintain their Mycenaean characteristics.

But although they remained Mycenaeans, they lost their vigor. The hundred-year decline toward oblivion had set in.

Historians and archaeologists have been arguing for a hundred years about the cause of Mycenae's fall. The three major theories are these:

1. Invasion and conquest by the Dorian Greeks.
2. Invasion and destruction by the People of the Sea.
3. Internal troubles resulting from tensions and hatreds growing out of the Trojan War.

The Dorians were Greek-speaking people—more barbaric than the Mycenaeans—who lived in the northern section of Greece. They took their name from their eponymous hero Dorus. According to Herodotus, the Greek historian, the Dorians first invaded Mycenae ten years before the Trojan War. Their leader was Hyllus, who professed to be a son of Heracles. Heracles, incidentally, was the Don Juan of his time. He ranged far and wide, and people who claimed to be his son were all over the known world of that time.

In any event, the two armies agreed to settle the war by a personal duel between Hyllus and Echemus, king of the Arcadians. Hyllus was killed. The Dorians withdrew, after promising not to attack Mycenae again for a hundred years. They came back in the years after 1100 B.C., using iron weapons to defeat the Mycenaeans and to take over the Peloponnesus as the Mycenaeans themselves once supplanted the still earlier settlers in this region.

This current view of Greek prehistory seems to rule out the Dorians as the cause of the widespread trouble in 1200 B.C.

The theory that the destruction was caused by wars with the People of the Sea is based largely upon historical guesses. No one knows who the People of the Sea were and where they came from. At one time there were claims that they were really the Mycenaeans.

All that is known of these mysterious seafarers is that they seem to have lived on the southwest coast of Asia Minor. They are mentioned in Hittite and Egyptian records as far-ranging traders. They became so strong in time that they destroyed the Hittite power in northern Turkey and smashed the coastal cities of Syria and Palestine. Then, in the time of Ramses III (1198–1167 B.C.), the People of the Sea were audacious enough to fight a sea battle with the Egyptians in the Nile Delta. An account of this defeat is carved on the walls of Ramses III's temple at Medinet Habu in Egypt.

After this defeat, the power of the People of the Sea declined, and we hear of them no more. However, since their period of greatest power coincides with the destruction throughout the Greek Mycenaean world, some have used this as circumstantial evidence that these mysterious sailors burned the Greek cities.

In no case did the People of the Sea (sometimes called the Peoples of the Sea, which implies a confederation) settle or try to control the lands they sacked. The attacks seemed to have been either to wipe out enemies and potential economic rivals or just to engage in plain piracy.

Eliminating these two possibilities, we fall back on the claim that the burning of cities in 1200 B.C. was caused by internal troubles arising from hatreds generated during the Trojan War.

For one thing, there was resentment between those who fought the war and those who remained behind and tried to supplant the absent warriors. We see two good examples of this in Homer: the plot of Aegisthus against Agamemnon in Mycenae; and the attempt of the various princes to force Penelope, the wife of Odysseus, to accept one of them as king of Ithaca after Odysseus was presumed lost.

Menelaus was bitter and lost his spirit. In the *Odyssey* Homer describes the visit of Telemachus, Odysseus' son, to Sparta. Menelaus tells the young visitor:

> Here too I have no joy as lord of my possessions. . . . Would I were here at home with but the third part of my wealth, and they were safe today who fell on the plain of Troy, far off from grazing Argos. But no! And for them all I often grieve and mourn while sitting in my halls.

Achilles' son was also very bitter, and others were angry over the division of the spoils. In addition, the normal jealousies of the different city-states, set aside for the war, now came to the fore. Argos, in particular, resented the power of Mycenae and Tiryns, since it was the older city.

We must also consider the economic impact of the Trojan War. Trade—which supported the Mycenaean cities—naturally fell off in wartime, and it is possible that some of these cities undertook to re-establish their wealth by preying on their neighbors.

All this points to almost continual civil war, which sapped the economic and physical strength of the Achaean Greeks. It caused the abandonment of the interior cities and a movement toward the coast.

Although there are many conflicting views about this unhappy period, the ancient historians were in surprising agreement about the time. They placed the final fall of Mycenae and the Mycenaean cities at eighty years after the return from Troy. The date of Troy's fall is controversial, of course, but striking an average between the various claims gives us somewhere around 1100 B.C. as the date of the second and final Dorian invasion. Kontorlis placed the fall of Troy at 1200 and the Dorian invasion at 1120 to get the eighty-year difference. Other guesses—and that is all they are—have varied as much as a hundred years from these dates. Carl Blegen's chronology gives the fall of Troy as 1260 B.C.

Kontorlis pictures the Peloponnesus at this time as exhausted and in chaos. "It is natural," he wrote, "that this would incite the Dorians and other tribes of the northwest. This invasion probably took place either peacefully, or after fighting, and was spread over decades."

There is no question about the Dorian takeover—or the return of the sons of Heracles, as it is also called, since the Dorians traced their ancestry to the famous strong man.

The archaeological evidence shows that after 1100 B.C. or thereabout, the Mycenaean civilization ended. The chamber and beehive (tholos) tombs were abandoned. A different type of pottery appeared. Iron—formerly a curious luxury—came into use in weapons. J. E. Jakovidis, in *Mycenae-Epidaurus*, says, "The ingenious, daring Mycenaean warriors, craftsmen and tradesmen were now succeeded by the new arrivals, dull, plodding farmers without any political ambitions or interests beyond the boundary of their farms."

The oceangoing ships stopped coming into the harbor. The Minoan-trained artists ceased beautifying the walls. The great citadels turned into ruins. It seems incredible that such a great and powerful people could collapse so quickly, but history is full of similar national tragedies. When a people lose faith in their leaders and the will to fight, they are an open target for a lusty invader.

The years between the coming of the Dorians and the beginning of Greek history in 776 B.C. are dark years. Even the legends and traditions are scant in this period. Archaeology is not much help either.

Greek history is dated from 776 B.C. because this is the date of the first Olympiad, the beginning of the Olympic Games and of record keeping in Greece. The later historian Herodotus had to rely on meager tradition and Homer to piece out the prehistory of his country.

As far as the citadel at Mycenae was concerned, the Dorians seemed to have burned and totally destroyed the acropolis with its palace of the king. Some sections of the great wall of the Lion Gate were knocked down, but the main sections of the walls seem to have remained intact. The city, except for the acropolis, continued to be occupied, probably by a mixture of Mycenaean and Dorian people. Some Mycenaean-type pottery continued to be made, but the great culture died rapidly. Nobody cared anymore.

During the first years of the Dorian invasion, refugees poured into other sections of Greece. This caused an enormous increase in Attica and boosted its major city, Athens, into an important cultural and political center. At the same time many fled across the Bosporus Strait into what is now Turkey and swelled the Greek Ionian settlements along the Aegean seacoast.

As Mycenae, Asine, Nauplia, Tiryns, and the other Mycenaean centers withered away, Argos grew in importance. It was more centrally located in the Plain of Argos and better situated for a capital. Tiryns and Mycenae both continued to be occupied and appear to have kept their independence as cities, although under Dorian control.

Although the cities and the people themselves decayed, the glory of the old Mycenaean world was kept alive by ballads and songs. The stories of Achilles, Odysseus, Troy, Agamemnon, and the curse of the House of Atreus were too stirring to be forgotten. These songs were composed by the wandering singers who traveled from place to place, literally singing for their supper.

Studies of the Homeric epics have given rise to the theory that there were originally eight or ten different songs. Then sometime between the eighth and tenth centuries, an editorial genius combined them all into what today are called the *Iliad* and the *Odyssey*. One nineteenth-century German investigator claimed that sixteen separate songs were combined to make the *Iliad*.

Current scholarship leans to the view that the *Iliad* is an original composition, but may be based upon earlier songs, as Shakespeare based his plays upon earlier plays and stories. Tradition gives this poet the name of Homer, but nothing authentic is known about him. The tradition that he was blind may have arisen from the description of the blind bard Demodocus, who sang of the Trojan War at the banquet for Odysseus in the *Odyssey*.

The *Iliad* and the *Odyssey* were not written down until the sixth century, which means that they were handed down orally for as long as three hundred years. This does not necessarily mean that they were altered in the long years of oral recitation. I can recall once listening to a talking chief tell the history of his island in the Pacific. He had at his side a very old man. Every time the talking chief was doubtful about any part of his story, he stopped and consulted the old man.

I inquired later and was told that the old man had been the talking chief in his younger days. The present chief kept consulting him to ensure that he was telling the story exactly as it had been handed down.

The *Iliad* has been called the bible of Greece, for it was not only an epic tale but also a recitation of Greek ideals. As such, it kept alive the glory of Mycenae through the dark ages between the fall of the Homeric period and the rise of the great Classical Age.

Nothing more is heard of Mycenae and Tiryns until the Persian Wars. The first war with Persia ended in the Greek victory at Marathon in 490 B.C. This was followed by the second Persian War, when Xerxes invaded Greece to avenge his father's defeat at Marathon. At first Xerxes was victorious, wiping out the three hundred Spartans under King Leonidas at the pass of Thermopylae. But this was followed by his disastrous defeat at the hands of the Athenians in the sea battle at Salamis; then the remainder of the Persian forces were defeated on land at Plataea in 479 B.C.

It is in this final battle of the Persian Wars that we again hear of Tiryns and Mycenae. Schliemann writes in his book on Tiryns:

> Tiryns . . . together with the town of Mycenae, sent four hundred men to the battle of Plataea. Consequently the name of the Tirynthians was enscribed, together with those other Greeks who took part in the battle, on the golden pedestal of the tripod which the Spartans offered to Pythian Apollo at Delphi.

He goes on to say that this aroused the jealousy of the Argives of Argos, since they took no part in the battle. Also, they had started to fear Tiryns again. There was a slave revolt inside the walls of Tiryns, and the city was still in the hands of the slaves.

The Argives attacked Tiryns. The slaves held out for some time, but were starved out in a siege. Then, "shortly after 468 B.C., the Argives are said to have destroyed the town, ruined a portion of the surrounding cyclopean wall, and forced the Tirynthians to move to Argos. According to other accounts, the Tirynthians fled to Epidaurus."

What remained of Mycenae suffered a similar fate for the same reason. Schliemann quoted Professor J. P. Mahaffy to this effect:

> No one seems to have found any difficulty in the statement of Diodoros, which Pausanias [the second-century Greek writer] repeats, that the town of Mycenae was destroyed by the Argives after the Persian Wars. I fancy most scholars, when they first come to attend to it, are surprised that the ancient city of Mycenae should have lasted so long . . . and yet have made so little figure in later Greek history.

He goes on to say that the names of the Mycenaeans were enscribed on the same tripod pedestal as the Tirynthians and the other Greeks who fought in the final battle. This tripod was later taken to Constantinople, where it was still on display in Mahaffy's day. Actually the list did not include individual names, as some have claimed; it only listed the cities. However, this proves that both cities were still in existence as independent units as late as 470 B.C.

Here is what Pausanias, in Book II, says:

> But I shall give the cause . . . why the Argives afterwards expelled the Mycenaeans. . . . The Argives destroyed Mycenae through jealousy, for

when the Argives remained neutral at the invasion of the Medes [Persians], the Mycenaeans sent to Thermopylae eighty men. This brought them destruction by inciting the Argives.

Another theory to explain the destruction of Mycenae and Tiryns by the men of Argos is that Sparta and Argos had clashed in each city's desire to be dominant in the Peloponnesus. By wiping out these two strongly fortified cities, the Argives removed threats to themselves. An alliance of either Mycenae or Tiryns with Sparta would have doomed Argos.

In addition, all the refugees from Mycenae and Tiryns who did not flee to Attica were moved to Argos. This enlarged the city, making it stronger and better able to withstand a Spartan attack.

At this point the great citadels at Mycenae and Tiryns ceased to be inhabited. Villages, farms, and orchards continued in the vicinity, but the cyclopean walls were deserted. This had happened before—notably in 1200 B.C. People returned then, but this time the desertion was permanent.

The cyclopean walls were too huge and strongly built to disappear. They remained for the next five hundred years little changed, as Greece itself underwent tremendous changes. We hear no more about Mycenae until Pausanias wrote his *Descriptions of Greece* in the second century A.D. It was his comments on the burial of Agamemnon that led Schliemann to the shaft graves which held the golden masks.

The awesome walls were an object of wonder to the Greeks of the Classical Age, as they are to visitors today. But it was Schliemann's astonishing discoveries that revived interest in Homer's Greeks.

But although Schliemann was the most colorful of the archaeologists who have worked to uncover Mycenaean secrets, he was but one of many investigators who have dug in these ancient sites.

10

LATER EXCAVATIONS

Stamatakis, who had so much trouble with Heinrich Schliemann during the German's explorations at Mycenae, was rewarded for his suffering by being made director of antiquities for the archaeological museum. He came back to Mycenae later and opened the sixth shaft grave overlooked by Schliemann. This grave contained the bodies of two men, bringing the total number of bodies found to nineteen. Here is the breakdown of bodies to graves:

Grave I, three women.

Grave II, one man.

Grave III, three women, two children.

Grave IV, three women, two men.

Grave V, three men.

Grave VI, two men.

These are the current determinations. Schliemann mistakenly identified some of the women's bodies as young princes. The greatest treasures were found in graves IV and V.

Although Schliemann has the honor of finding the largest amount of treasure and of reviving interest in the Mycenaean past, he was by no means the first to dig there.

After Pausanias in the second century A.D., the next to take an interest in Mycenae was Lord Elgin, who collected many Greek treasures for the British Museum in the mid-nineteenth century. He took some objects from the Treasury of Atreus.

The first excavations were made in 1841, when the Greek Archaeological Society uncovered the Lion Gate and the entranceway. No other work was done due to lack of funds. Also, no one recognized the importance of the site until after Schliemann made his discoveries in 1875. Actually, Schliemann did not have much interest in Mycenae. His heart was in Troy. He only dug in Mycenae because of its association with Troy and because he was temporarily barred from Troy after he stole the Trojan treasures.

Even after he found the shaft-grave treasure (which weigh over thirty pounds of gold), he was not interested in continuing work at Mycenae, which he considered worked out. He transferred his expedition to Tiryns and then back to Troy, returning later to Tiryns again.

After Stamatakis' excavations of Shaft Grave VI in 1877, the work at Mycenae was taken over by the Archaeological Society with the digging under Charles Tsountas, who conducted the work from 1880 to 1902.

Tsountas moved higher up the hill than Schliemann and Stamatakis, who had confined their work to the vicinity of the Lion Gate. Tsountas found the ruins of the palace atop the acropolis and discovered the passageway leading to the underground spring that furnished water to the citadel. He also moved outside the walls entirely and discovered ruins of houses and a number of tombs.

After Tsountas, work languished until resumed by Alan J. B. Wace in excavations made between 1919 and 1923. Wace returned in 1939, but was interrupted by the outbreak of World War II. He resumed his work in 1950 through 1956. He was followed by William Lord Taylor, who directed excavations until 1966.

In addition to this work directed by foreign archaeologists, the Greek Archaeological Society had resumed operations at Mycenae. At first this was restoration work only. The society replaced some of the slabs marking the ring of Grave Circle A, paved the approach to the Lion Gate, and built some steps up the first part of the ramp to facilitate the climb for tourists who were now flocking to the site.

In 1951 the society began work restoring the top of the Tomb of Clytemnestra, which had been originally uncovered by Schliemann's wife Sophia. The top had fallen in. The stones were replaced by following the angle of the remaining stone.

But in digging around the edges of the tomb, the restorers hit a low rock wall that appeared to be part of a large circle. The excavators sensed that they had found another grave circle, like that uncovered by Schliemann inside the walls. The following year, J. Papademetriou and George E. Mylonas uncovered Grave Circle B, the work of excavation continuing through 1954.

This grave circle was outside the walls, about 425 feet west of the Lion Gate. The low wall encircling the grave site was made of two parallel circles of stones, with the space between them filled with dirt and rubble.

Inside, the excavators found fourteen deep shaft graves like those of Grave Circle A. In addition, there were ten shallow graves of more common people than the royalty buried in the deeper shaft graves. The shaft graves are dated between 1600 and 1650 B.C. The shallow graves are of a later date. In all, the graves contained twenty-five people—fifteen men, six women, two girls, and two boys.

The graves in Grave Circle A were numbered for easy reference. Those in Grave Circle B were given letters. The most curious grave was number P, which was completely different from all the others. It was a small chamber made of stone slabs with the roof coming up to a point. It has been dated at about 1450 B.C., or two hundred years later than the shaft graves in the same location.

The treasure buried in Grave Circle B is not as rich as that Schliemann found in Grave Circle A. This has led some observers to think that Grave Circle B is somewhat older than A, although both are of the same basic period.

Weapons, vases, swords, and other objects were found in the various graves. The most beautiful object was a rock-crystal bowl carved like a duck's body with the neck curved back to create a handle for the bowl. Another unusual object was a piece of amethyst with a man's profile carved on it in a cameo manner. Other objects were of gold, bronze, and ivory. They were all interesting, but were not spectacular like the golden masks found at the other site.

Just south of Grave Circle B, excavations by Alan Wace uncovered four buildings dating from the thirteenth century B.C., which would be in the closing years of Homer's Greeks. As was customary with all the houses uncovered, these were named for objects found in them, like the famous House of the Warrior Vase inside the city walls.

One of these was called the House of the Shields, because several miniature models of shields, carved from ivory, were found in it. The houses sat on a raised area and a stair led between them to the road below.

The next house is called the House of the Oil Merchant. It revealed a long passageway, lined with huge jars that once held oil. Abutting this house was another built on the same design. It is called the House of the Sphinxes, because several ivory plaques engraved with sphinxes were found in it.

Although they have been called houses, it appears from the relics found in them that these were commercial stores. The rooms found were the business parts of the buildings. The merchant and his family probably lived upstairs on the second level, as was discovered later in Thera.

The buildings were substantial, indicating that trade was good. Later discoveries, including a hearth for heating the oil and other finds, indicate that the oil merchant may have been a perfumer instead of just a seller of oil. The oil was heated and blended on the site to create popular scents.

The other two buildings probably belonged to merchants dealing in popular religious objects. No shavings were found to indicate that the work was done on site. So they may have been importers, dealing in a wider selection of objects than just those made of ivory. In any event, their business sharpness is shown by the location of their stores. They were beside the road leading to the Lion Gate, where everyone had to pass by their shops.

Extensive explorations and excavations have also been done at nearby Argos. Very little of the Mycenaean period remains here. Argos, unlike Mycenae and Tiryns, was never deserted. The continual occupation destroyed the older buildings and foundations. The more interesting remains are of the Classical Age and the Roman period.

The big find after Mycenae and Tiryns was at Pylos, the kingdom of

Nestor. Like Troy, the site of Pylos had been lost for centuries, and archaeologists had put forth claims for three separate sites. Then, in 1939, Carl Blegen and K. Kourouniotis, working with a joint Greek-American group, uncovered the ruins of a great palace at Epano Englianos in Messenia province. This is on the west coast of the Peloponnesus, parallel with Sparta.

Blegen had earlier amassed a great reputation for his work at Troy. There he proved that Schliemann had been wrong in identifying Troy II as Homer's Troy. Blegen identified it as Troy VIIa, and authorities generally are in agreement.

Preliminary excavations at Epano Englianos justified Blegen in announcing his belief that this was Nestor's Pylos. The work was halted by World War II, but Blegen came back in 1952 with the Princeton University expedition.

Nestor's palace, like those of Mycenae and Tiryns, was built around a megaron divided into three portions. The entrance was from an interior courtyard. The first section was a porch, then a vestibule, then the main throne room. The floor was covered with colored squares. In the center was the same raised hearth found in Mycenae, surrounded by four pillars that supported the roof. The section of the roof directly above the hearth was open to permit smoke to rise. A throne was set in one end of the megaron. In front of it was a square decorated with a large octopus.

According to Pausanias, Neleus, father of Nestor, was run out of Thessaly in the early thirteenth century. He came to Messenia in the Peloponnesus, where a cousin gave him a strip of land on the coast. Here Neleus built the beginning of the palace of Pylos, which his son Nestor inherited.

The *Iliad* identifies Nestor as a very old man, the most aged of all the Achaean kings. Tradition says that he lived to be a hundred years old. He had been a very strong man in his youth, and in his old age loved to brag about his athletic accomplishment. At the same time, he is pictured as a very wise man and a good king. Pylos, long after Nestor's death, was destroyed in the same mysterious fashion as the rest of the Mycenaean world. Its survivors are supposed to have fled to Athens.

The most far-reaching discovery at Pylos was the uncovering of the royal archives. Here Blegen found over a thousand clay tablets inscribed with Linear-B writing. Examples of Linear-B writing had first been discovered by Sir Arthur Evans at Knossus. Then additional examples were found in Mycenae. Earlier, another example of a written script had been discovered and named Linear A. It was called "linear" because it was written in horizontal lines instead of columns like some other ancient languages.

A tablet from the Heraklion museum on Crete shows an example of Linear-B script, which proved to be an archaic form of Greek.

Evans put considerable effort into attempts to decipher Linear B, but failed. Since he withheld publication of photographs of the Knossus tablets, others were prevented from working on the problem.

After the discoveries at Mycenae, there was considerable work done at deciphering the strange language, but without success.

Then the remarkable discovery of the thousand tablets of Pylos by Blegen stimulated interest in the problem. Among those inspired by the discovery was a young British architect named Michael Ventris. Ventris began an intense study of the tablets.

It is almost impossible to determine an unknown language without some kind of guide. The Egyptian hieroglyphics could not be deciphered until a French soldier found the famous Rosetta Stone. This stone contained a message in three languages, including Greek. By comparing the Greek text with the hieroglyphics, Egyptologists unlocked the secret of the ancient Nile picture writing.

When such comparisons are missing, the unknown writing may never be read. This has happened in Mohenjo-Daro, the lost city on the Indus River in Pakistan. No one has been able to decipher the markings found there. Most felt that the same would be true of Linear A and B scripts. Up to the present time, they have been right about Linear A, but Ventris broke the secret of Linear B.

In writing based upon the Roman alphabet, each letter stands for a sound. A short combination of these sounds make up a syllable or part of a word, and one, two, or more syllables make a word. Ventris decided that the length of the lines did not indicate that each mark in Linear B was a single letter. Since the arrangement of the signs indicated to him that this was a syllabic type of writing, he decided that each sign was a syllable.

In some very complex applications, he compared the different signs and worked out a syllabary. Various sounds were substituted, and it finally developed that the written language was an archaic form of Greek.

After working out the proper sounds for each syllable of the language, Ventris read, *Ti re pode, ai ke u, ke re si jo, we ke.* This is rendered into English as "Tripod caldrons of Cretan workmanship."

From this small beginning, he was able to read all the tablets at his disposal. Proof of the accuracy of his system lay in the fact that it fit all the tablets, producing intelligible sentences. Unfortunately, all the tablets—including those of Mycenae and Knossus—only dealt with lists of property. There was no literature and no political or legal documents. All were inventories only.

Although the decipherment turned out to be a severe disappointment in this one respect, the reading of Linear B proved that the Greek language was in use at Knossus in its final period. It also proved that the Mycenaeans ruled in Crete during the last years of Knossus.

The fact that all the Linear-B records found to date deal with business does not mean that there was no written literature or political records. These tablets were originally all unbaked clay and broke down when soaked with water. The only ones that survived were those burned in the great fires that destroyed the various palaces, which baked them into brick.

So we cannot dismiss the possibility that somewhere in unexcavated parts of the Peloponnesus there are undiscovered tablets that may yet reveal more of the mysteries of Mycenae.

11

VISITING MYCENAE AND THE ARGOLID

One of the most delightful trips that one can take is to follow the trail of the Mycenaeans through the various places that retain ruins from the days of Homer's Greeks. None are difficult to get to, but they are widely scattered. This involves travel by car and bus, and short air hops or ship tours. But all the major sites can be easily covered in a ten-day vacation. During the summer, students—who stay at the youth hostels scattered over Europe—flock to these historic places.

A full tour of the world of Homer's Greeks would start at the Mycenaean room in the National Historical Museum in Athens, then travel by excursion through the Plain of Argos, visiting the citadels of Mycenae, Tiryns, and Nauplia. The regular tours do not go to Pylos and Argos; for these sites, one has to arrange private transportation.

After the Argolid would come a boat trip (they range in length from three to seven days) to the Aegean islands. Ports of call on these trips include both Crete and the ruins of Knossus plus an especially awesome sail into the old volcano caldera at Thera.

Back in Athens from the boat excursion (the trip can also be made by air to Crete), the next step in a complete tour of Homer's Greece would be a flight to Istanbul in Turkey. Here you must arrange a 180-mile automobile trip to the ruins of Troy. It is quite a long ride, but well worth it to walk where Helen of Troy walked, look into the pit where Schliemann found the Treasure of Priam, and stand where the Wooden Horse brought doom to the city.

The best way to see the Argolid is to rent a car in Athens and drive. There are excellent roads, one of which is a toll road. The only shortcoming of a drive-yourself tour, or of joining the hordes of students who put on knapsacks and hike over Greece, is that you may miss a lot that a guide could point out. I have found that the best thing is to take one of the one-day guided tours, which go by bus from Athens, then later go back and see the country at your leisure.

The Argolis tour, which includes Mycenae, costs around $25 and includes lunch. It leaves Athens at 8:30 A.M. and returns about 7:00 P.M. It is quite comfortable in an air-conditioned bus with English-speaking guides. The only drawback is that they never let you stay as long as you would wish in any one place. Also, they do not stop at all the places, but only point them out as you drive by. There are several companies who make these tours, and all are excellent for the hasty traveler or someone who wants to get an idea of what to come back and see.

The Argolis tour (as the Greeks call it) drives through the industrial section of Athens and then skirts the coast, where you see Salamis, the island where the great naval battle that decided the Second Persian War was fought. You pass Eleusis, where the famous mysteries were conducted (and where there is a delightful wine festival today), and skirt the Gulf of Corinth to the Corinth Canal. This deep, sea-level ditch separates the Greek mainland from the Peloponnesus.

All the tours stop here for a look at the canal. Before the canal was dug, the ancient Greeks would unload their ships and cargo, pulling them along a special road to cross the narrow section of land that then connected the Peloponnesus to Greece. On the return tour, remaining sections of this ancient road are visible from the bus.

After the canal, the tours stop at old Corinth for a walk through the Roman period ruins. The highlight here is the Agora, where Saint Paul preached to the Corinthians. In the background the towering columns of an even more ancient temple to Apollo look down upon the Christian elements of the ruins.

From Corinth the road goes west to Mycenae. Although the different tours may take different approaches to lessen the crowds at the citadel, the usual approach is to stop at the Treasury of Atreus first. This is the giant beehive tomb, sunk into the side of a hill on the road to the citadel.

From the tomb site, there is a splendid view across the valley to Mycenae itself. It occupies the top of a comparatively low hill between Mount Prophet Elias and Mount Zara. The entire expanse is clearly visible, from the sections where the low city crowded the base of the hill up through the successive circles of walls to the acropolis, where the king's palace was located.

After the tomb stop, the bus continues to the parking lot—which is always jammed, for Mycenae is one of the most popular tours in Greece. You walk from the bus to the fenced entrance of the citadel site. There are admission fees to all Greek archaeological sites. These vary in price, from about fifty cents to $1.50, but are included in the guided tours. For those on their own, the ticket office sells guidebooks that quite adequately describe the site, its history, and things to be seen. In general, Greek guidebooks (which are available in three languages, including English) are very complete. Unless one is an archaeologist, they include everything the casual visitor will want to know or see.

The guided tours only take their visitors inside the Lion Gate to Grave Circle A and then wait for those who want to climb the hill, through the ruins of houses, to the acropolis.

The tour then returns to the bus by the same entrance road past the ticket stand. However, those who have studied the maps in the guidebooks can get a much more rewarding return by leaving the path at the foot of the Lion Gate wall and bearing left along a footpath that winds downhill. This takes the visitor past the crumbling thalos tomb of Aegisthus and close by the so-called tomb of Clytemnestra. Clytemnestra's tomb is almost a replica of the Treasury of Atreus, but is not so large or well preserved.

Then, climbing one of the sometimes difficult footpaths back uphill, you come to the Grave Circle B at the edge of the site fence. Here are shaft graves and ruins of houses.

From the Grave Circle B, a short walk back toward the citadel takes one to the houses of the Shields, Sphinxes, and the Oil Merchant (or perfumer).

A line of tourists climb through the shattered remains of houses on their way from the Lion Gate to the acropolis at Mycenae. Mount Prophet Elias is in the background.

The area surrounding Mycenae is dotted with tombs and relics, including a stone bridge remaining from the original Mycenaean road that connected all the cities in the Plain of Argos. These are not covered by any of the tours. A local guide should be used for visits to these, for it is easy to get lost.

From Mycenae, the tour goes to Nauplia, a delightful town on the Gulf of Argos. This is the lunch stop before proceeding on to Epidaurus, the ancient sanctuary of Asclepius. On the way to Nauplia, the bus passes the ruins of Tiryns, but does not stop.

These tours have arrangements for one- or two-day trips. Those who take the two-day tour leave the bus in Nauplia, having the afternoon, night, and morning next day free. They then pick up the next day's bus tour when it arrives about 1 P.M. The hotel is included in the tour fare.

This arrangement permits you to pick up a taxi in Nauplia and visit Tiryns in the afternoon or the next morning. It is a very short distance away on the road to Argos.

Since Tiryns is not on the regularly scheduled tourist routes, the visitor has the place pretty much to himself. In a half-day visit, I saw fewer than ten people there. This is in addition to an archaeological team that is digging in the lower-citadel section of the ruins. Tiryns is not as impressive as Mycenae, but still well worth a visit.

After Tiryns, another ten miles brings you to Argos. Argos is a very interesting town, but has little of the Mycenaean period remaining. As you turn back to the coast, there are several old Mycenaean ruins, at both Asine and Lerna, on opposite sides of the bay at Nauplia.

Nauplia itself is a total delight. It has no Mycenaean sights, except the museum. In Mycenaean times Nauplia was a swamp. After the Venetians captured the area in A.D. 1388, the swamp land was filled in to make the present townsite on the shore. The town is dominated by the huge Palamidi Rock, which is over 600 feet high. The sprawling walls of the Venetian Palamidi fortress covers the elevation. From here one has a wonderful view of the Gulf of Argos. Just offshore is a tiny islet covered entirely by a small fortress called Bourdzi. For a while this beautiful place was a hostel, with boats going to the shore at Nauplia every hour. The last time I was there I was told that plans were under way to turn it into a casino.

Nauplia is a favorite summer resort, and at night all the cafés move their tables and chairs out in the middle of the street. Superb Greek food is then served under the stars. The cool breezes blow in off the Gulf of Argos, and Bourdzi is floodlighted.

The archaeological finds from Mycenae and Tiryns have been taken to the National Archaeological Museum in Athens. Even so, the museum in Nauplia is worth a visit. It is housed in an old Venetian naval arsenal building. One unique exhibit is the only set of full bronze armor that has been found in Greece. It dates from the fifteenth century B.C.

Back in Athens, the National Archaeological Museum is a must stop. It can be visited first. However, it is much more interesting and meaningful after one has seen Mycenae. The regular half-day guided tour of Athens takes in the museum, but does not give one enough time. A longer visit is necessary to view its many wonders.

The museum is within walking distance of central Athens, where many of the tourist hotels are located. You can go when it opens at 10 A.M. and stay until they close the doors at 5 P.M. You can take cameras into the museum, as well as to all the archaeological sites. However, in all cases, you will be charged an extra admission ticket for the camera. If you have two cameras, then you will need a ticket for each of them. These camera tickets are not included in the price of your tours.

The Mycenaean Hall, directly in front of the museum entrance, houses all the treasures found in the excavations. The golden masks are mounted on black velvet backgrounds, against which the gold gleams in awesome beauty. The frescoes, notably the women driving a chariot and dogs closing in on a wounded boar, are arranged on the wall. Other cases display the rings and the dove-handled cup of Nestor. Of special interest are the beautiful Vaphio cups with their embossed pictures of Minoan-dressed men catching bulls. The Warrior Vase with its scenes of marching men from the Homeric period is another interesting exhibit.

All the Mycenaean treasures are in this hall, except for a Theran room, which is being reconstructed on the second floor. This reproduces, complete with wall painting, a room from Akroteri, the city that was covered Pompeiilike with ash when Thera exploded.

Side trips to Crete to see Knossus and the Heraklion museum can be made by air. It is an hour's flight. The one-day tour leaves at seven in the morning and returns at midnight. Included are two meals—lunch and dinner—at one of the better hotels in Candia (Heraklion) and a bus tour of the site of Knossus, followed by a visit to the museum. The afternoon is free—you can wander around town or rent a car to drive to some of the other Mycenaean sites on the island.

Another way to visit Crete is by cruise ship. These sail from Piraeus, the port of Athens, several times a week. The shortest is the three-day cruise, which takes in a short stop at Mykonos, Rhodes, Crete, and Thera.

A bus tour of Knossus is part of the cruise. It is not an extensive ruin,

The Minoan ruins at Knossus can be visited by excursion cruise boats or by a short air trip from Athens. This shows the south entrance of the Palace of Minos as partially restored by Sir Arthur Evans.

and what one sees is mainly restorations—although very impressive. Whole buildings and pieces of walls with broken columns rear up majestically. These are all reconstructions, paid for by Sir Arthur Evans, who spent more than a million dollars for the work. The wall paintings found in the ruins have all been removed to the Heraklion museum, and the ones in the reconstruction areas of Knossus are copies which Evans had made and placed in the ruins.

The tour weaves through these awesome halls, and it is easy to see how the legend of the Labyrinth got started.

The Heraklion museum has the originals of the wall paintings from Knossus. Of special interest is the famous bull-leapers fresco, but this is only one of many treasures associated with Mycenae.

From Crete the cruise ship goes to Thera. There are no plane flights to the island, and the visitor is forced to go by boat. This is quite an awesome trip and extremely interesting, both for its Mycenaean associations and for the claim that this might well have been the model for the Lost Atlantis.

As the ship approaches the Thera group, the islands appear as a series of low black smudges against the horizon. But as the ship sails through the vanished sections of the islands into the enclosed waters that once were the central part of the land mass, the great, black, multilayer cliffs rise up directly out of the sea.

The town of Thera clings to the top of the high cliffs, startlingly white against the blackness of the volcanic cliffs and the deep blue of the sky.

There is no port. Ships anchor in the shadow of the cliffs and visitors go in aboard small lighters. There is a six-hundred step climb to the top of the cliffs, but donkeys and mules are available to give you a ride up.

Thera is visited by excursion boat. The town perches precariously on the edge of the volcanic cliff. The sea where the boats are anchored was once part of the island. The land was blown away in the tremendous underwater explosion that destroyed the major portion of the island.

The sight from the top is quite awesome. You can look down upon the cruise ships below, and across the water to the remnants of the exploded island. On one of these the volcano still smolders. Occasionally it tosses out rocks and smoke and often shakes Thera with earthquakes, but it has been 3,400 years since it really harmed anyone.

The Mycenaean ruins at Akroteri, just below the city of Thera, were not open to the public in 1980.

These are the major Greek Mycenaean sites. Troy, with its Mycenaean associations, is in Turkey. A visit requires flying to Istanbul, and taking a tour from there to Troy, about 180 miles away. There are no airports nearby, Troy being about midway between Istanbul and Izmir (Smyrna), where airports are available. It is not an extensive ruin, but is an extremely interesting one.

It has been 104 years since Schliemann first began to solve some of the mysteries of Mycenae. Since that time men like Stamatakis, Carl Blegen, Alan Wace, George Mylonas, William Dorpfeld, Sir Arthur Evans, William Lord Taylor, and others have chipped away at the curtain that hides the true story of Homer's Greeks.

They have revealed a lot, proving Homer right in many respects. Still, many mysteries remain for future archaeologists and historians to find answers to. Young people interested in archaeology will find Greece still a fertile field. Years ago we heard that Greece had all been worked out. Then we learn of new discoveries like the recent uncovering of the tomb of Philip of Macedonia (1978), proving that golden treasure and historic discoveries can still be made.

And the astonishing accomplishments of Michael Ventris, who worked from photographs to decipher Linear-B script, shows that one does not even have to be an archaeologist to make outstanding contributions to the uncovering of Mycenaean mysteries.

With such slow chipping away, perhaps someday we will know the whole fascinating story about what really happened at Troy and in the tragic halls of Mycenae.

Chronology

All prehistory dates are controversial.

5000–2600 B.C.	Neolithic (New Stone Age) culture in Crete.
2600 B.C.	Minoans settle in Crete.
2000 B.C.	The Ionian Greeks are first to penetrate into the present land of Greece.
2000–1700 B.C.	Minoans from Crete rule the Aegean Sea; period of great palace building at Knossus.
1700 B.C. (estimated)	Achaean Greeks are first Greek-speaking people to penetrate into the Peloponnesus, driving out the native pre-Hellenes.
1600 B.C.	Beginning of the Achaean rise to power and development of the Mycenaean culture.
1500–1400 B.C.	Estimated time of the destruction of Thera by an exploding volcano.
1400 B.C.	First destruction of Knossus; cause unknown.
1270–1260 B.C.	Peak of Mycenaean power; war with Troy. Time of the *Iliad*. (This date is not accepted by all authorities. Some date the war as much as a hundred years later.)
1100 B.C.	Fall of Mycenae from unknown causes.
479 B.C.	Tiryns and Mycenae furnish soldiers to help defeat Persian invaders.
468 B.C.	Argos destroys remainder of Mycenae and Tiryns.

A.D. 100 (circa)	Pausanias visits Mycenaean ruins.
1841	Archaeological Society excavates Lion Gate.
1875	Heinrich Schliemann begins excavations at Mycenae.
1876	Schliemann discovers gold masks.
1880–1902	C. Tsountas excavates at Mycenae.
1919–1923	Alan J.B. Wace conducts excavations at Mycenae.
1950–1956	Wace continues excavations.
1951–1954	J. Papademetriou and George E. Mylonas discover Grave Circle B.
1952	Carl Blegen resumes excavations started in 1939 at Pylus; discovers Linear-B archives.
1956	Michael Ventris announces decipherment of Linear-B tablets.

Bibliography

Alsop, Joseph, *From the Silent Earth*. New York, Doubleday and Co., 1959.

Blegen, Carl, *Troy and the Trojans*. New York, Frederick A. Praeger, 1963.

Chadwick, John, *The Mycenaean World*. London, Cambridge Press, 1966.

Christoforakis, J. M., *Knossos*. Candia, Crete, Christoforakis, 1978.

Doumas, Christos G., *Santorini*. Athens, Editions Hannibal, not dated.

Grant, Michael, *The Ancient Historians*. New York, Charles Scribner's Sons, 1970.

Homer, *The Iliad*. Edited by Leaf, Lang, Myers. London, Macmillan, 1889.

Jakovidis, S. E., *Mycenae-Epidaurus*. Athens, Ekdotike Athenon SA, 1978.

Kitto, H. D. F., *The Greeks*. Baltimore, Penguin Books, 1951.

Kontorlis, Konstantinos P., *Mycenaean Civilization*. Athens, J. Makris S.A., 1974.

Lang, Andrew, *Homer and His Age*. London, Longmans, Green, 1906.

Leaf, Walter, *Homer and History*. London, Macmillan, 1915.

Schliemann, Heinrich, *Mycenae*. New York, Scribner, Armstrong & Co., 1878.

Schuchhardt, Karl, *Schliemann's Excavations*. London, Macmillan & Co., 1891.

Taylor, William, *The Mycenaeans*, New York, Frederick A. Praeger, 1964.

Vaughn, Agnes Carr, *House of the Double Axe*. New York, Doubleday and Co., 1959.

Index